Inferno at Petersburg

INFERNO
AT
PETERSBURG

BY

Henry Pleasants, Jr.

AND

George H. Straley

CHILTON COMPANY—BOOK DIVISION
Publishers

Philadelphia & New York

Published in Philadelphia by CHILTON COM-
PANY, and simultaneously in Toronto, Can-
ada, by AMBASSADOR BOOKS, LTD. Library
of Congress Catalog Card Number 61-6473.
Manufactured in the United States of America by QUINN & BODEN COMPANY, INC.,
Rahway, N. J.

To the Memory of the Officers and Men
of the
48th Pennsylvania Volunteer Regiment

who accomplished so much so well with so little

Contents

Inferno at Petersburg

Prologue

An air of expectancy hung over the crowd surrounding the roped-off enclosure on the Virginia hillside. It was April 30, 1937, and a thrilling spectacle was about to take place. We occupied a space beside the platform on which the Governor of the Commonwealth and other high officials sat. With us were Senator and Mrs. Wesley Hale, of Massachusetts, and Major Carter R. Bishop, the last remaining Confederate veteran in Petersburg, all of whom had done much to bring about the event we had come to witness—the dedication of the National Battlefield Park at Petersburg.

It was here, on July 30, 1864, that one of the most extraordinary feats of military engineering up to that time had been accomplished—the explosion of a mine under the fort blocking the Union advance toward Petersburg and Richmond. That project had been the brain child of a humble lieutenant colonel commanding the 48th Pennsylvania Regiment of Volunteers, most of whom were coal miners from Schuylkill County, Pennsylvania. It had been successful in the face of skepticism, ridicule, jealousy, and obstructionism on the part of Union officers of the highest rank. It should have ended the War Between the States. . . .

A bugle sounded. Instantly, with a flash of flame and a deafening roar, the whole hillside before us was blotted out.

1

Through a cloud of black smoke we caught glimpses of flying timbers, clods, and what appeared to be human bodies hurtling skyward, then falling back into the enormous crater scooped out by the blast.

We had barely recovered from the shock of the explosion when, through the slowly clearing haze, we began to see blue-uniformed figures moving up the hill in broken lines and surrounding the crater. There was no slightest semblance of military formation, little evidence of leadership. Several officers raced back and forth, waving their sabers and endeavoring to bring some sort of order out of the existing chaos.

Again the bugle sounded. The troops in blue quickly formed into companies and, with the precision and cadence of veterans, marched off down the hillside. The first phase of the re-enactment of the Battle of the Crater had ended.

After an hour's intermission, the bugle sounded for the third time. The roped-off area was promptly cleared. Soldiers marched up to the crater, broke ranks, and disappeared behind piles of loose earth or into the crater itself. A crackling of musketry sounded from a line of breastworks at the crest of the hill above us.

"Watch now!" cried Major Bishop. "Confederate sharpshooters are picking off Union men in the crater. Confederate artillery will lob a few shells into the mass. After that—"

It all happened just as he had said. Even though we knew that those smoking balls that dropped with uncanny accuracy where they were aimed were bundles of oil-soaked rags, the real horror of what had occurred here, seventy-three years before, was vividly seared on our minds and hearts.

Presently, from over the crest of the hill above us, marched a full regiment of gray-clad figures in perfect battle formation, their bayonets glistening in the early afternoon sunlight. A few paces ahead of each unit marched its commanding officer with drawn saber. Well in advance of the regiment rode a heavily bearded officer closely followed by three of his staff.

"That's General Mahone," explained the Major. "Those troops are the boys of the Virginia Military Institute. They're making the great counterattack that saved Petersburg. Aren't they superb? But why wouldn't they be? See who is watching every move they make—that mounted officer up on the crest—that's General Robert E. Lee on Traveller."

The counterattacking force moved swiftly down the hill and drew up in perfect formation around the rim of the crater. Suddenly, a white shirt raised on a musket fluttered above the milling mass of Union troops. The bugle sounded Recall. The dedication ceremonies were over. . . .

I had been privileged to see a reincarnation of what I had many times envisioned in my imaginings, and for me this episode, dredged from the not-so-distant past, had a peculiarly personal fascination. For the man who, on that July day in 1864, had held briefly in his hands the fate of this nation, and had seen his high hopes crumble in bloody disaster, was my cousin, Lieutenant Colonel Henry Pleasants. All my life I have tried to learn as much about him as I could—have tried to piece together, from family correspondence, personal memoirs, and official documentary data, the real story of the Petersburg Mine as it involved him. The result, more than anyone else's, is his own story.

HENRY PLEASANTS, JR.

3

1

Inevitable Hour

In mid-June of the year 1864, the most strategically important city in America was Petersburg, in the County of Dinwiddie, in the Confederate State of Virginia.

On the vast chessboard of the War Between the States, it was a stubborn pawn blocking the path of the Union armies driving toward the Rebel capital, a great sprawling obstacle on the road to Richmond, twenty-two miles to the north. Its fate, and the fate of Richmond, were joined inextricably, so that the massive storm clouds gathering over it cast into chilling shade the pin-studded map on the wall above Jefferson Davis's desk in the stronghold of the Confederacy.

Normally a community of approximately 18,000 residents, Petersburg in that year was a heavily armed camp. On three sides—north, east, and south—it bristled with fortifications, abatis, and earthworks. Mile after mile of entrenchments encircled it, their labyrinthine corridors patrolled by raw militia hastily alerted for combat. From the north, seasoned troops, pulled out of the lines that had successfully held the enemy at bay in Bermuda Hundred, were arriving to reinforce the city's defenses. The grim stage was being set for a sequel to the tortured Wilderness Campaign of the preceding month. For now Lieutenant General Ulysses S. Grant—who had vowed to "fight it out on this line if it takes all summer," but had butted in vain against General Robert E. Lee's lines securing the frontal approaches to Richmond—had fixed his cold and calculating eye on Petersburg. And Petersburg was bracing itself against expected assault.

How soon the assault was to come, what was to be its magnitude, or what it would cost in human life and human suffering, no one knew. Nor did anyone know, in mid-June of 1864, that the climax of the assault would be reached in a fantastic operation unlike anything that had been seen in this war—indeed, unlike anything ever before seen in the history of warfare on the North American continent.

The storm that broke over Petersburg in the early summer of 1864 had long been anticipated. As early as 1862, a series of stoutly constructed redans or batteries, connected by infantry parapets of high profile, had been erected in a broad sweeping semicircle two miles outside the city. These defenses had been planned deliberately and were built with extreme care by the generous use of conscripted civilian and slave labor. They were garrisoned by a single brigade under the command of a former Virginia governor turned soldier, Brigadier General Henry A. Wise, whose command included many willing but inexperienced home guards. Any tactical report on the position of Petersburg, up to the middle of June, 1864, would have noted that it was strongly fortified but thinly manned.

The city had had stormy times in the past. Founded as a trading post in 1733 by one Peter Jones, the place had first been called Peter's Point. It was incorporated as a town in 1748 and the name changed to Petersburg. During the Revolutionary War period it was occupied briefly by the British before they were driven out by Lafayette. In 1815 it was almost totally destroyed by fire, and rebuilt. Twenty years before the Civil War, geographers were calling it "a first-class town, giving an appearance of enterprise and wealth."

Much of the enterprise had gone into making Petersburg, on the Appomattox River, an important railhead and port of entry, and from this achievement had come much of the wealth. Since early colonial times, the city had been a primary shipping point for the vast tobacco plantation area surrounding it. It was served by no less than four major railroads—the Virginia Central, the Lynchburg, the Danville, and the Weldon. The latter connected with Wilmington, North Carolina, 225 miles away, where Confederate blockade runners unloaded their supplies for direct shipment northward.

It was these vital arteries of transportation that made Petersburg, lying so near to the nerve center of the Confederacy at Richmond, a prize tremendously coveted by the Union forces. Through Petersburg flowed the materials that supplied the Army of Northern Virginia. If the lifeline were severed, Richmond and the troops defending it would be starved into surrender. Repeatedly during the spring of 1864, units of the Army of the Potomac and the Army of the James attempted to destroy the railroads. Early in May, Brevet Major General George A. Custer's cavalry raided Beaver Dam Station and tore up ten miles of Virginia Central track. Other cavalry troops under Brevet Major General A. V. Kautz harassed the Weldon Railroad. These sporadic attempts hindered but did not choke off the vital flow of matériel and supplies into Petersburg and Richmond. They were mostly piecemeal forays, and served principally to annoy the enemy and detract his attention now and then from the main drive on Richmond.

For Richmond at that time was the target. It was only after the rugged six weeks in the Wilderness, after the bloody horror of Spottsylvania and the bitter repulse at Cold Harbor, that the Union attack was shifted to Petersburg. Actually, that city could have been taken as early as

May 10, while the Wilderness Campaign was still in full swing.

On that date, when the Army of the Potomac was sweeping down through Spottsylvania, the Army of the James, commanded by Major General Benjamin Franklin Butler, was preparing to march on Richmond from the south. On the night of May 9, two of Butler's corps leaders, Major Generals Q. A. Gillmore and William F. (Baldy) Smith, strongly urged him to lay a pontoon bridge over the Appomattox and attack Petersburg. Butler was persuaded, but shortly thereafter changed his mind, about-faced toward Richmond, was driven back, and forced to retreat into the peninsular shelter of Bermuda Hundred. He has been criticized for indecisiveness, but perhaps undeservedly; he had been instructed to cooperate with the Army of the Potomac in its drive on Richmond, and he lacked the inspired initiative to strike out on his own. Nevertheless, on May 10, Petersburg had scarcely more than 2,000 men in its earthworks. It was a sitting duck that could have been bagged easily.

A month was to go by before Butler had another chance. On June 9, he sent Generals Gillmore and Kautz on a joint infantry-cavalry expedition to destroy the railroad bridge across the Appomattox and capture the city. Somehow the defenders of Petersburg got wind of the plan. Every able-bodied youth and man in the city was pressed into duty with General Wise's brigade, and when Gillmore took stock of the situation he concluded that his own force was not strong enough for the job, and turned back. A few miles away, at another sector of the perimeter of entrenchments, Kautz's cavalry attacked with some success, and advanced to a point near the city reservoir before they were routed by artillery.

There were other attempts, and at least one propitious occasion when no attempt was made. That was on June 17.

By then Petersburg was a tougher nut to crack, for its garrison was being steadily strengthened by veteran troops from the lines before Bermuda Hundred, hastily deployed to meet the full-scale assault that Grant was then launching. General G. K. Warren was assigned to swing his Fifth Corps in a wide arc around the city, and to attack from the south, where it was most vulnerable. But for some reason this promising thrust was never carried out.

It was on this same day that Brigadier General James H. Ledlie's division, in Burnside's Ninth Corps, smashed against Petersburg's outer fortifications in the first display of the main assault force. Ledlie's troops pierced the line, but ran out of ammunition and were compelled to withdraw. The time was to come, only a few weeks later, when Ledlie would be handed one of the most important assignments in the Petersburg Campaign, and history would be obliged to record his bungling of that job as one of the most glaring examples of ineptitude in the annals of the war.

There were no further favorable opportunities. Thanks to the alertness of General Pierre G. T. Beauregard, who, perhaps sooner than any other Confederate commander, sensed the magnitude of Grant's push on Petersburg, the anxious city was now defended by 10,000 Rebel soldiers. For the next four days, they took one punch after another, and gave better than they took. And at the end of that time, Grant counted casualties, chewed meditatively on a cold cigar, and wisely concluded that Petersburg was not to be taken by storm. Pushing regiment after regiment into a great semicircle around the city, he settled down to a long siege.

It remained, then, for an unsung unit of Burnside's Ninth Corps to cover itself with glory and ashes in the next phase of the Petersburg Campaign—the mining of the fortifications. Strange indeed was the coincidence that brought the 48th Pennsylvania Veteran Volunteers, made up almost en-

8

tirely of anthracite miners from Schuylkill County, Pennsylvania, to the closest point of contact with the enemy earthworks. Whatever trick of destiny had brought this about, the chance had to be exploited.

And destiny had turned up the man to exploit it. He was a man without precise counterpart in the entire Army of the Potomac, a man whose character and temperament were compounded of unknown parts of courage, imagination, energy, enthusiasm, and ruthlessness. He was fiery and cold and hard as steel, and his dark brown eyes were lit with an impetuous lust for action. He was Lieutenant Colonel Henry Pleasants, commanding officer of the 48th Pennsylvania Volunteers. He had been a mining engineer, and there was coal dust in his hair.

2

Second Lieutenant

During the period of the War Between the States, probably no one knew Lieutenant Colonel Pleasants better than one of the fellow officers who served under him throughout the entire four years of conflict. This was Major Oliver Christian Bosbyshell, who summed up his appraisal of the regimental commander in these words:

"He was a soldier of true grit, possessed of more than ordinary ability as an engineer—ability that he displayed many times during the campaign from the Rappahannock down to Petersburg, in the erection of temporary fortifications which he required the regiment to build every night, and the lives of many men were saved through this precaution."

There is no doubt that Colonel Pleasants was exceptionally well qualified to lead the troops under his command. These were volunteers from Schuylkill County, Pennsylvania, an important center of the hard-coal industry at that time, and most of them were miners. Pleasants knew these men, their families, their backgrounds and the communities they came from, and the nature of the toil they had been used to since their early teens. Between these men and their commander were a rapport and a mutual respect not often to be found in the military units of this or any other war. The relationship had a significant bearing on the Petersburg episode.

Pleasants himself was a mining engineer, with a background of education in the public schools of Philadelphia. In 1856, five years after his graduation from Philadelphia's Central High School, he went to work for the Western Division of the Pennsylvania Railroad. He was employed as senior assistant engineer in the construction of the Pittsburg & Connellsville Railroad, in the progress of which he completed the famous Sand Patch Tunnel, one of the largest engineering projects of its time.

Many of the peculiar characteristics of temperament that made Colonel Pleasants a daring and colorful leader in combat are explained by his family background. He was of English ancestry, direct descendant of forebears who came to America from Norwich about 1665 and established a large tobacco plantation on the James River, at Curle's Neck. These antecedents were Church of England stock, but in Virginia they embraced the religious faith of the Society of Friends. For this action they were prosecuted, but the stubborn attitude with which they resisted the Church's efforts to punish them helped pave the way for eventual passage of the Toleration Act, which granted religious freedom in the American Colonies.

The quality of stubbornness was handed down through succeeding generations of the family. Convictions, and the courage to act in accordance with them, seem to have been a portion of the birthright of every member. As early as 1771, John Pleasants—grandson of the original Virginia plantation owner—directed in his will that the more than 500 slaves he then owned should be set free after his death, "if they chuse it when they arrive at the age of thirty years." He was recognized as the first emancipator of slaves in Virginia, if not in the United States. His son Robert, on whom he apparently exerted great influence, organized the Abolition Society in Virginia, became its first president, and was far ahead of his time in advocating schools for Negroes.

11

Another son, Samuel Pleasants, who abandoned plantation life to engage in mercantile pursuits in Philadelphia, was persecuted for his adherence to Quaker principles during the Revolutionary War. With his father-in-law, Israel Pemberton, and a score or more of other Philadelphia Friends, he was banished to Winchester, Virginia, as a suspected Tory, and remained in exile for more than a month before General Washington personally intervened and ordered his release.

However, the pacifist convictions of the Pleasants family in Philadelphia dwindled rapidly after the American Revolution. Beginning with the War of 1812, the family name has appeared on the roster of armed forces in every conflict up to the present day. And of those who bore the name, none did so with greater gallantry than Lieutenant Colonel —later Brigadier General—Henry Pleasants.

He was born February 16, 1833, in Buenos Aires, Argentina. His father, John Pleasants, was a Pennsylvanian who had renounced a tame clerkship to engage in the far more exciting business of smuggling arms and ammunition to Argentinian insurgents. These revolutionary elements were seeking to overthrow the notoriously cruel dictator, Juan Manuel de Rosas, and set up a democracy. It was a cause that deeply stirred the active sympathies of the young clerk. Deeper and more personal stirrings were to follow, when, in the course of his contacts with the wealthy estate owners of the Argentine who were financing the uprising, he met Sylvia Naveis, the beautiful daughter of a Spanish nobleman. He married her and settled down in Buenos Aires— and of this marriage the boy Henry was born.

John Pleasants died in 1846, leaving instructions that his son should be sent to the home of his favorite brother, Dr. Henry Pleasants, in Philadelphia, to be educated. Unescorted, the 13-year-old Henry made the long voyage by sailing vessel. He never went back to South America.

Doctor Pleasants was a highly successful practitioner, and at that time held the post of Physician to the Port of Philadelphia. He had lived in Hamiltonville, West Philadelphia, before moving into his spacious residence at Radnor, on the Main Line west of the city. Here he housed a sizable family of his own, but he and his wife, Emily, welcomed his namesake nephew into their home with sincere warmth and affection. Young Henry was shortly enrolled in the Southwest Grammar School, where his progress was severely handicapped by the fact that he spoke only Spanish. Fortunately, his uncle had made two visits to Argentina—had, in fact, practiced medicine there for some time—and spoke Spanish fluently. This helped considerably to mitigate the immediate difficulties of communication in the household, and in due time the language barrier was surmounted in school, for the boy learned English rapidly. He did not, however, make an impressive showing as a scholar, in either grammar or high school.

He was a sensitive child, with a shy manner that derived both from gentle breeding and transposed environment. The shyness inevitably invited the attentions of ruder schoolmates, who mimicked his courteousness and made him the target of rough and embarrassing pranks. They were to learn that beneath the layers of modesty and refinement smoldered a hot Latin temper that could billow into consuming flame under extreme provocation.

Such an extremity occurred on the Southwest Grammar School playground one morning at recess. It had rained the night before and the ground was muddy in spots. Henry, standing alone in a corner of the yard and watching other youngsters at their games, was suddenly jostled and tripped by several older boys. He fell painfully into a puddle, and when he struggled to his feet he discovered that his clothes were covered with mud. The smoldering spark burst into scorching flame. Lashing out with his small fists, he pummeled one of his tormenters to the ground, then attacked the other two with such fury that they fled in dismay. Other boys gathered around and cheered him. There was no more trouble after that.

In Philadelphia's Central High School, the boy's scholarship improved noticeably, although his marks conveyed no indication of future greatness in any category of life. At no time would he have been voted the youth most likely to succeed. Nevertheless, he finished second in his class of seventeen, and was graduated in February, 1851, with a Bachelor of Arts degree. Then, as now, Philadelphia Central was the only high school in the United States empowered to confer degrees.

It is strange that a young man who as a student had shown so little aptitude for mathematics, should have been attracted to the field of engineering. But from the very beginning of his job as a surveyor's assistant with the Western Division of the Pennsylvania Railroad, Henry Pleasants displayed a remarkable liking and capacity for the work. The position was one which his uncle had helped procure, and he was determined to make good. By 1853 he was senior assistant engineer of the railroad, and a year later he was involved in a project which was to bring him at least contemporary fame, as well as experience that would stand him in good stead years later.

Under a spur of the Allegheny Mountains in western Pennsylvania, railroad engineers proposed to run a 4,200-foot tunnel. Young Pleasants, just turned 21, was placed in charge of some of the most important phases of the project. A major problem in construction was that of providing adequate ventilation. Singlehanded, Pleasants solved this problem in a manner that made engineering history. From the surface of the mountain range he sank four perpendicular shafts to meet the line of tunnel excavation at appropriate points. These shafts ranged from 120 to 200 feet in depth. When the work of tunnel excavation had progressed as far as one of the shafts, a fire was built at the base of the shaft. The superheated air drew all accumulated foul air out of the tunnel, enabling the workmen to proceed without danger of suffocation.

The Sand Patch Tunnel, as it was named, was under construction for three years. About the time it was completed, the chief engineer and president of the road, O. W. Barnes, was dismissed for some reason, and there were strong rumors that Pleasants would be asked to succeed him. Pleasants' reaction was typical of his nature. As on the school playground when he was beset by bullies, the smoldering fire of his temper flared forth. Barnes had been his friend. Out of loyalty to that friend, he must refuse not only to replace him; he must refuse to stay any longer in the employ of a company that had acted so unjustly. He resigned his position with the railroad immediately.

Back at Rockland, the comfortable home of Uncle Henry and Aunt Emily Pleasants, the jobless assistant engineer of the Sand Patch Tunnel found the respite that was due him. He had been working hard, and for several weeks he enjoyed the luxury of idleness, doubtless making plans for his future but communicating them to no one. Then one day came a visit from Franklin B. Gowen of Pottsville, Pennsylvania. Gowen was a bright young fellow of contagious enthusiasm. He had worked for a time on the Sand Patch Tunnel, and had struck up a friendship with Pleasants that was to last a lifetime. Later on, he was to become president of the Philadelphia and Reading Coal and Iron Company, and both he and Pleasants, the latter as chief engineer of the same company, were to become deeply involved in the investigation of the infamous coal field terrorists known as the "Molly Maguires."

15

"Pleasants," Frank Gowen said earnestly, "you must come up to Pottsville. That country is bursting with coal, and a good mining engineer can make a fortune."

Pleasants was persuaded. He found Pottsville a rough boom town filled with grimy Irish miners, coal prospectors, get-rich-quick industrial promoters, and a good many free-lance engineers like himself. It was a dreary, barren place, but it seethed with a deep-stirring activity that fired the young man's imagination. He rented a room, hung out a sign advertising his services, and soon found that good mining engineers were indeed in great demand. Gowen was right; the mountains around Pottsville were bursting with anthracite. All that was needed to bring these black diamonds to the surface was a safe and practicable system of deep-shaft mining. And deep-shaft mining became Pleasants' specialty. As one successful project after another was completed, he began to see that Gowen must also be right about the fortune that was to be made. Yet his real fortune lay in another direction.

Like every other mining man in Pottsville, Pleasants read the community's principal newspaper, *The Miner's Journal.* On several occasions he met the editor of this thriving publication, and one day he was introduced to the editor's daughter. Her name was Sallie Bannan, and she was everything that Henry Pleasants had ever dreamed of. He courted her in the manner that now characterized everything he undertook—impetuously, impatiently, with a zeal that brooked no interference. Early in that year of 1860 they were married.

It may be safely assumed that in the six months following his wedding, Henry Pleasants found the greatest happiness of his life. Sallie was cultured, socially accomplished but domestically inclined, and very calmly, very deeply in love with her high-strung husband. They moved into a modest home on Washington Street that soon became a center of charming social entertainment for many of the important people in Pottsville's booming coal industry. Young Henry Pleasants, everyone said, was a mighty lucky fellow—a man on the way up.

They were wrong. He was a man on the way down— down to the depths of overwhelming tragedy. Sallie Bannan Pleasants was pregnant in the summer of that year; the baby was expected around Christmas. In mid-October she suddenly became ill. Roused by her moans of agony in the early hours of morning, her husband sprang from his bed, ran out into the dark street to pound frantically on a neighbor's door, then raced a couple of blocks away to summon a physician. For several hours Sallie's life hung in the balance. Then, as suddenly as she had come into his life, she was gone.

He was like a wild man. Caged in by his excruciating grief, he flailed savagely against the bars that isolated him in a personal tragedy no other human being could share. The frightening fury lasted for forty-eight hours. Then he collapsed in numb exhaustion, stunned and helpless, and his friends took over the duties and responsibilities he was incapable of facing. At the burial service, when Sallie's coffin was being lowered, it took four husky young miners to restrain him from hurling himself into the grave.

It would be months before he was himself again—and he would never truly be his old self. Time, of course, would heal the wound, but the scar was to be forever ineffaceable. He went back to Rockland, and in the quiet of the big house with its peaceful surroundings he found a healing therapy for his frayed emotions. Nothing would ever be quite the same for him, but under the kindly ministrations of these two people who were more real than the memory of his true parents, he could recover some portion of a rationalism that had almost fully deserted him.

As his health returned, he fidgeted with the problem of

what to do next, where to turn. It was a question vastly complicated by a national unrest that had been brewing for a long time. The Christmas holidays that year—the season in which his child was to have been born—were heavy with the gloom of disunion. South Carolina had seceded. Other states would follow. There was to be a war.

Early in the new year, Henry Pleasants sat before the big fireplace in the living room one evening and heard his Aunt Emily say an astounding thing. Years later, knowing her sweet and kindly nature, her love of beauty and order, her abhorrence of violence, he would wonder how she had found the courage to say it, or the understanding to know that it needed to be said.

"Henry," he heard her say, "have you given any thought to enlisting in the army? Maybe, after what you have been through, it would . . ."

It was as far as she could go. He said nothing for a long time, watching the flames curl over the logs in the fireplace, lost in a reverie all his own. Then he rose and kissed her gently on the forehead. The problem had been solved, momentarily at least. It was a way out of the personal cell of his loneliness, a way back to the world of people, of action, of accomplishment. It would be a gray world, a cold world —never the place of color and warmth that it had once been for him. But it was a way out. He could not stay on at Rockland forever.

The Pottsville he returned to was in a state of spirited excitement. Fort Sumter had been fired upon. "Father Abraham" had issued his call for volunteers. Militia were being organized, and Pleasants promptly enlisted for three months' service as a second lieutenant in the "Tower Guards." His unit went into training at Perryville, Maryland. Mustered out in July, he re-enlisted immediately in the 48th Pennsylvania Veteran Volunteers, and the following month was appointed captain of Company C. War was now in full swing, and he had committed himself to its precarious fortunes—in the private hope, not to be divulged until years later, that he would be killed in action and thus released from his burden of bitterness and pain and futility.

But he had a rendezvous at Petersburg, and he was destined to live.

3

A Soldier Learns

It would not be unreasonable for the average student of history to assume that the 48th Pennsylvania Regiment, in the War Between the States, shared in the common run of battle experiences, forced marches, camp discomforts, scant rations, epidemics, extremes of cold and heat, and similar trials of military campaigning endured by other active regiments in the Union Army. However, as actual war records show, the 48th was called upon to perform a series of tasks that were exceptionally difficult. One of these was a six-month tour of patrol duty at Lexington, Kentucky, where almost evenly divided citizen factions of North-South sympathizers were creating considerable tension and occasional strife. Kentucky was a borderline state, and the job of preventing any radical outbreak of anti-Union elements within its boundaries, or any infiltration of Confederate troops from without, was an important one.

To accomplish this delicate task would appear to require, more than almost anything else, a background of culture, refinement, and education far beyond that of the average coal miner. Even though the officers of a regiment composed largely of miners might be fortunate enough to have such a background, it would seem utterly impossible for those officers to influence their regiment personnel sufficiently to produce satisfactory results in less than several

months. That this was accomplished in a phenomenally short time is in itself proof of the rigid military discipline that formed the very backbone of the 48th. To this was added the almost idolatrous devotion of the men to their officers, and of the officers to their men. Together, both discipline and devotion were built up through a series of hardships, dangers, and sufferings almost beyond comprehension.

Shortly after its formation in the summer of 1861, the 48th Pennsylvania Volunteer Regiment, commanded by Colonel James Nagle, was made a unit of the Ninth Corps under Brigadier General Ambrose Everett Burnside. The first official assignment of the regiment was to occupy two large earthworks at Hatteras Inlet, North Carolina. These had been built by the Confederates to assist English blockade runners in getting through to Pamlico Sound and thence to the commissary depots with supplies of arms, food, and clothing. As this entire area was frequently buffeted by violent storms of hurricane intensity, the post was probably one of the least desirable of any occupied by a unit of the Union Army. But the 48th stood the winter of 1861–62 amazingly well. Also, it performed a most valuable engineering feat in erecting a causeway of barrels filled with sand so that the two forts, which had been captured by General Ben Butler and Commodore Silas H. Stringham in a joint Army-Navy assault, could be used satisfactorily.

The following March, 1862, Burnside ordered Colonel Nagle to have six companies of the 48th accompany the fleet on its expedition against New Bern, N. C. Officially, this was the regiment's first battle, but since it did not actually come under fire, Colonel Nagle pointedly neglected to have the word "New Bern" inscribed on the colors, until actually ordered to do so by General Burnside, who felt that the hard work the regiment had performed during the expedition should be recognized.

The Second Battle of Bull Run, August 29–30, 1862, was the 48th's first actual engagement under enemy fire. Although suffering 152 casualties in killed, wounded, and missing, the regiment was later described by one historian as *"conspicuous on this day for the persistence with which it held its ground when assailed and the gallantry with which it advanced to the attack."*

The Battle of Chantilly, on September 1, was fought in the midst of a terrific thunderstorm. Historians generally agree that had General John G. Pope been given the proper support, he would have become a people's hero of the hour. Unfortunately, had this happened, it would have lessened the popularity of General George B. McClellan, who already had been put on a pedestal by politicians and the press.

In the Battle of South Mountain, September 14, in which the Union troops under Burnside and his Ninth Corps paved the way for the great Battle of Antietam, the 48th distinguished itself for its coolness and courage under extremely difficult conditions. Six days later, Captain Pleasants was promoted to lieutenant colonel.

It is significant that after South Mountain was taken, General Burnside personally accompanied this regiment in the pursuit of the retreating Confederates, although this necessitated sharing the discomforts caused by delay in the arrival of the commissary. One morning he was seen making his breakfast on a single ear of corn, which he had roasted himself. The loyalty and devotion of the 48th Pennsylvania Regiment to its corps commander seems to date from this comparatively minor incident. As will be shown later, these feelings were reciprocated by General Burnside who, on November 9, 1862, was promoted to the high post of Commanding General of the Army of the Potomac.

The Battle of Fredericksburg on December 13, 1862, ended in a rather dismal failure for the Union Army.

Briefly, the Confederates occupied Marye's Heights, key point of the Union attack. This they had made as nearly impregnable as possible. After successive troops under French, Hancock, Howard, and Humphrey had stormed this stronghold unsuccessfully and with frightful losses, Burnside endeavored to persuade his division commanders to support his plans, already outlined, to make one more attempt, in which he would lead the attack in person. Wisely, this was not done.

Following the failure at Fredericksburg, the Union Army settled down in winter quarters. On January 26, General Burnside bade farewell to those he called his "well-tried associates" of the Ninth Corps. The 48th, however, was eventually detached from the Ninth Corps and ordered to report at Fortress Monroe for duty at a destination not made known to any but the higher-echelon officers.

The detached service to which the 48th was assigned began with boarding the steamer *John A. Warner* at Fortress Monroe, at 3 A.M., March 26, 1863. Five days later, after almost constant travel over various railroads, punctuated by stops at York, Mifflin, Altoona, and Pittsburgh, in Pennsylvania, and at Newark, Columbus, and Cincinnati, Ohio, the regiment reached its unforeseen destination at Lexington, Kentucky.

Now for the first time the troops realized that General Burnside had been removed from leadership of the Army of the Potomac, and had been appointed Commanding General of the Army of the Ohio; in taking over this new post he had requested that his beloved Ninth Corps be allowed to accompany him on an extraordinary mission. Lexington was a most important city, and the assignment of the 48th there, on April 3, with Colonel Joshua K. Sigfried as provost marshal, was a high honor as well as a great responsibility for Lieutenant Colonel Pleasants and his mining men.

The first undertaking of the 48th after its arrival was to construct comfortable barracks in a location that would enable the companies to assemble speedily in the event of a raid on the city by Morgan or Pegram, whose units had been making the lives of Union sympathizers miserable in other towns of the state. A second task was to improve the old fortifications at Fort Clay by constructing earthworks and other additions necessary for security. The third was to devote many hours to regimental as well as company drills; this not only kept the men actively employed but also made a salutary impression on the citizens of Lexington.

One serious lapse in regimental decorum and discipline occurred on the first pay day following the troops' arrival, when nearly every enlisted man proceeded to get gloriously drunk on a brand of corn whiskey for which Kentucky has been famous since colonial days. The ensuing jamboree landed a large number in the guardhouse and removed the privileges from several companies. Pleasants, who was acting provost marshal at the time, handled the situation with a tact and dispatch that paid large dividends in citizen confidence and respect.

On April 29, Colonel Sigfried was relieved as post commander by Colonel Byrd of the 1st Tennessee Regiment, which had been ordered to replace the 48th Pennsylvania on provost guard duty. Within forty-eight hours, however, these orders were canceled. It was later discovered that the citizens of Lexington had petitioned the commanding general to permit the 48th to remain on duty in their city, and the request had been granted. The rest of the Ninth Corps moved on into East Tennessee.

When on September 8, 1863, orders came relieving the 48th of duty in Lexington, a letter prepared and signed by ninety prominent citizens eloquently expressed their appreciation of the conduct of the regiment. One paragraph reads:

"Coming among us strangers, you have from the first to last treated us as friends; and while you have been compelled to act with firm vigor against the open and secret enemies of the government, your administration of the affairs has been tempered with justice and humanity, and such good order and discipline has been maintained among your troops that all citizens who in good faith have desired to live peaceably and obedient to law, have felt perfect security from all outrage or even injury or injustice."

During the regiment's six months of detached service in Lexington, Lieutenant Colonel Pleasants had managed to find some time for personal interests beyond the duties of military occupation and troop discipline. In July, he had been appointed provost marshal general of the Twenty-third Army Corps, with headquarters in the city, and enjoyed a status socially acceptable to the finest families in the community, with the result that he and some of his fellow officers were frequently feted in the homes of various prominent citizens.

One such citizen was Hiram Shaw, a wealthy merchant to whose warehouses had been shipped the first secret consignments of arms for Union sympathizers there. His house had been thrown open to the officers as a headquarters of lavish hospitality. To Colonel Pleasants, the standards of gracious living observed in the Shaw mansion were especially gratifying. The people he met there spoke his own unforgotten language of culture and refinement, and shared his appreciation of the beautiful things of life, and in their company he was proud to recall an interesting family association with the city. His own uncle, Thomas Franklin Pleasants, had visited Lexington en route to New Orleans alone on horseback from Philadelphia, in 1816, and had been entertained at the home of the great statesman, Henry

Clay. Also, there were many things in this environment that brought back memories of earlier days in his grandfather's hacienda in Buenos Aires.

One evening, Colonel Pleasants attended a dinner party at the Shaw home. As the guests assembled in the magnificent parlor with its glittering chandelier, Persian rugs, and fine old furniture, he was introduced to a beautiful young girl, whose frank excitement in being allowed to attend such an occasion among grown-ups added to her charm. Combined in her were all the delicate womanly graces, plus an aura of rugged individuality that suggested pioneer ancestry. Yet there was something ingenuously childlike in the way she confided that Uncle Hiram had asked her mother to allow her to fill an empty place at table. Henry Pleasants was completely captivated. Before the evening was over, they were chatting and laughing as if they had known each other as jolly friends for years. Suddenly, for the first time since the death of his beloved Sallie, the young officer realized that while there was not and never could be anyone to take her place in his heart, he had found in Anne Shaw the person who could lead him out of the slough of despondency—something that all the excitement, anxiety, responsibilities, and dangers of military service had not been able to do. Within a month they were engaged, although Anne was but sixteen at that time, and when his orders came to leave Lexington with his old command, he had a new objective—to give proof of his own real worth as a leader in the eyes of a splendid woman who loved him as he loved her.

The 48th left Lexington on September 10, although Pleasants himself departed for special duty on August 18, by order of Brigadier General Hartsuff, on whose staff he was provost marshal. He did not rejoin his old command until it was on its way eastward. Colonel Sigfried's orders were to move the First Brigade as quickly as possible to Knoxville, Tennessee, by way of Cumberland Gap, a distance of more than two hundred twenty miles. The objective was reached in nineteen days, and considering the fact that the route traversed rugged mountain country, rain-swollen streams, and roads often hub-deep in mud, the accomplishment was phenomenal. Added to the hazards of terrain was the uncertainty of the location of enemy units, which were trying to prevent General Burnside from concentrating a large force of Union troops in Knoxville.

The schedule of daily marching was rigorously followed. It began before dawn and continued steadily until late in the morning, when a rest of three hours was taken. In this way, the troops were not exposed to too great fatigue on any one stretch. Describing his personal experiences during this long march, Colonel Pleasants wrote to his Uncle Henry and Aunt Emily that he had actually learned how to take a reasonably comfortable nap while bracing himself properly in the saddle.

On the twenty-first of September the brigade reached Morristown, moving from there by train to Knoxville. There, the sagacity of Major General Ambrose Burnside became apparent. The Confederate Lieutenant General Longstreet was making a rapid advance on Knoxville with 28,000 men. Including a few regiments of green troops, designated as the Twenty-third Army Corps, the total number of Union forces was but 8,000. In addition to Longstreet's numerical advantage, his troops were in fine condition. Furthermore, he had excellent railroad communication from Chattanooga to Loudon, about 29 miles from Knoxville. Apparently, the odds were all in favor of the Rebels annihilating Burnside's forces.

Burnside proved equal to the occasion. He withdrew his troops across the Tennessee River at Loudon, then took up the pontoon bridge the engineers had made for this purpose. He next destroyed a locomotive and four cars by running them into the river so that the Confederates could not use them. Next, he withdrew his supplies into Knoxville as rapidly as possible, while his troops, including the 48th Pennsylvania, were posted at Campbell's Station to oppose the Confederate advance. The attack of the Confederates was repulsed during the entire day of November 16. That night, the 48th withdrew to Knoxville, which was promptly invested by the Confederates under Longstreet.

The canny Burnside now made the best possible use of Colonel Pleasants' mining troops, and a line of earthworks was thrown around the city in a great semicircle. Engineers dammed up two culverts of the East Tennessee and Virginia Railroad, so as to make a formidable moat just below the position occupied by the Ninth Corps. Union picket lines were extended as far beyond the circle of fortifications as possible, and a night surprise by the Confederates was prevented by setting fire to several small frame houses near by when an assault was threatened.

Longstreet was desperately anxious to capture Knoxville and Burnside's troops, as this might easily prove the turning point in the war. Also, it would to some extent counterbalance Lee's failure at Gettysburg the preceding July. He made a tremendous attack on the fortifications on November 29, but the 48th had prepared for this by clearing the forest in front of Fort Sanders. Between the stumps left by the axe-men, telegraph wire had been stretched like a great spider web. When the attacking rebels ran into this they became utterly disorganized. In justice to the Confederates, it must be noted that they continued advancing to the fort, and the flags of the 13th and 17th Mississippi and 16th Georgia Regiments were actually planted on a corner of the ramparts. But they got no farther.

A large number of prisoners were taken by the Union forces, but General Burnside wisely returned these to their own lines, rather than jeopardize his own meager food supply. Longstreet was too wary to settle down to a starvation siege, and, accurately informed that reinforcements under Sherman, Howard, and Granger were on their way to help the plucky Burnside, he withdrew his army on December 5.

The congratulatory letter of President Lincoln to General Grant at his headquarters in Chattanooga, was relayed by Grant to Burnside. It was so expressive of the President's full appreciation of, and gratitude for, the accomplishments of the preceding weeks that it must be given here:

"Washington, December 8, 1863

To Major General Grant:—

Understanding that your lodgment at Chattanooga and Knoxville is now secure, I wish to tender you and all under your command, my more than thanks, my profoundest gratitude, for the skill, courage and perseverance with which you and they, over so great difficulties have effected that important object. God bless you all!

A. Lincoln"

Perhaps it is evident from this that Lincoln felt his confidence in Burnside as a leader well justified, notwithstanding the circumstances that had prevented Burnside from accomplishing what he had hoped to do at Fredericksburg. No doubt Lincoln now realized, for the first time, that his removal of Burnside as Commander of the Army of the Potomac had been brought about largely through pressure on the part of regular army top-ranking generals who venomously opposed Burnside whenever opportunity afforded. Perhaps he had learned the truth about the way in which McClellan had refused to give Burnside the support he actually had available—some 15,000 men in reserve—after Burnside had made his famous capture of the bridge at Antietam and had seen an almost unbelievable opportunity

29

to win a victory that might end the war. Many regular army officers had never lost sight of the fact that Burnside was the son of a humble tailor. He had graduated from West Point in 1847, as a first lieutenant. In 1853, he had resigned from the army to enter business as a manufacturer of fire-arms, since he had invented an exceptionally practical breech-loading rifle. In 1861, he had offered his services to the Union cause, and his leadership of volunteer forces had been outstanding, as attested by his rapid advancement over the heads of his former West Point colleagues. Naturally, he was not popular with them, and the support they could have given him at critical times was not always forthcoming.

The 48th Pennsylvania Regiment, after leaving Knoxville December 7, 1863, experienced one of its most severe periods of hardship. On the ninth it reached a small village which had been entirely stripped of provisions by Confederate troops just twenty-four hours before. Rations were scanty. The weather had turned bitter cold, and the roads over which food and clothing had to be transported became frozen bog holes. There was also the anxiety of possible attacks by the enemy. On the 17th there were a few skirmishes near Blaine's Cross Roads.

In spite of these hardships, the 48th was the first regiment of the Ninth Corps to secure the necessary three-fourths quota of re-enlistments in order to qualify for one month of veteran furlough. January 11, 1864, orders were received directing the regiment to proceed to Pennsylvania and report through the Governor to the Superintendent of Recruiting for furlough and reorganization.

Out of the hills of Tennessee, back to the hills of Kentucky, marched the 48th—and in Lexington, Pleasants hurried to the home of Hiram Shaw, to hold Anne in his arms for a brief moment, and reassure her of his love. On January 25, he entrained with the regiment for the long journey east, arriving February 3 in Pottsville to find that the whole town had turned out for a roaring homecoming celebration.

Then, for a few sadly sweet nostalgic days and nights, he was back at Rockland, in the big house with Uncle Henry and Aunt Emily, telling of what he had seen and experienced. In the telling, as he sat by the fire in the quiet living room, his voice sounded harsh—to his own ears and to his listeners—like the voice of another person, a stranger. But when he laid a gentle hand on Aunt Emily's shoulder, and told her of Anne Shaw, the long-concealed light of recaptured youthful happiness brightened his face and brought warmth to his words. And for the rest of his stay the restraints of war were gone and he was like a boy again.

Fleeting and unreal as a dream, the furlough ended. Pleasants and the 48th Pennsylvania returned to the Ninth Corps, which was now in Virginia and was soon to be united with the Army of the Potomac for an all-out offensive against Lee's fortifications before Richmond. Unexpectedly, Colonel J. K. Sigfried was promoted to brigade commander, and Pleasants was appointed to replace him as commander of the 48th regiment. The appointment was made May 1, 1864. Next day, the Army of the Potomac crossed the Rapidan River. Ahead lay the Wilderness, Spottsylvania, Cold Harbor. And beyond them, only a few weeks and a few miles away, was Petersburg.

4

Sand in the Gears

From the time he herded his Army of the Potomac over
the Rapidan on May 2, until the bloody repulse at Cold
Harbor a month later, General Ulysses S. Grant had met
with bitter frustration. The highly touted hero of Vicksburg, invested less than two months with the supreme authority of General in Chief, had carried into the savage Wilderness Campaign the highest hopes of President Lincoln
and the citizens of the North. He was fifth in the line of
Union crusaders—successor to Meade, who had succeeded
Hooker, who had replaced Burnside, who had followed Mc-
Clellan. Grant had earned the reputation of a hard, stubborn, relentless fighter, and he had more than lived up to
that reputation in the two terrible Wilderness battles, and
at Spottsylvania Court House. In those three sledge-ham-
mer blows at Lee's army he had gambled for high stakes,
and his losses were profligate—more than 30,000 killed,
wounded, and missing in the brief span of eight days, May
5–12. Nevertheless, in bulldog defiance of the frightful attrition, he informed his superiors in Washington that "I
propose to fight it out on this line, if it takes all summer."
The words were not prophetic. On June 3 came Cold Harbor, with another 12,000 Union casualties; and suddenly,
while the Confederate lines still held, the force behind the
battering ram was spent.

It was a time for respite and recapitulation. Exhausted by five weeks of hammer-and-tongs campaigning, the stalled Army of the Potomac was sorely in need of this opportunity to recoup its strength. There was the temptation—and it was a beguiling one—to settle down to siege tactics and skirmishing. But this prospect was not to Grant's liking. He had thrown everything he had at the enemy, and it had not been enough. To make things worse, General Ben Butler's Army of the James had failed to execute the planned pincer movement on Richmond from the south, and was now being held at bay by Beauregard in Bermuda Hundred, twenty-four miles away. The Wilderness Campaign was at an end. It was up to Grant, the aggressor, to launch a new offensive —or lose face at Washington as his predecessors had done.

The General in Chief took two days to think it over. Then, from the sleeve of his battle-faded uniform, he played his last card. And presently storm clouds began to gather over Petersburg.

From June 5 to June 12, no one except the top brass of the Union army knew what was coming. Among the rank and file of the troops, engaged in digging trenches that they confidently expected would shelter them for months to come, rumors began to circulate, but they were vague and conflicting and no one wanted to believe them. Surely, so soon after Cold Harbor's frightful carnage, Grant could not contemplate another assault!

But on Friday night, June 10, the big news began to break. The Army of the Potomac was going to move—not into battle, but away from the enemy. Quietly the units were alerted, the word passing from corps to division, from brigade to regiment. It was to be a sneak-out maneuver, a trick to vex the enemy. Grant was up to something, although nobody seemed to know what. Nobody, at this stage, particularly cared.

In common with his men of the 48th Pennsylvania Volunteers, Lieutenant Colonel Henry Pleasants knew little of what was taking place. The Ninth Corps was relatively new in this theater of the war, having been officially transferred to Meade's command less than three weeks before. For this reason, the grapevine had shallower roots. But gradually these facts emerged: Grant was preparing to execute a mammoth flank movement; orders had been issued to evacuate the presently occupied area under cover of darkness on the night of June 12; the entire Army of the Potomac was clearing out, unit by unit, and heading south. The age-old question, the question enlisted men in uniform have asked each other from time immemorial, in all the armies of the world, went the rounds. "Where do we go from here? What's up?" The answer was only a few hours away.

Sunday, June 12, dawned on a scene of feverish activity that was successfully concealed from the enemy. Gear was assembled, rosters checked, tents struck, artillery limbered. Then, hours of waiting while the bright hot day wore on. Finally, twilight, dusk, star-rise—and suddenly the low-spoken order to march.

Down dark lanes through the woods, across fields, along a winding road layered thickly with dust, Burnside's Ninth Corps infantry trod quietly. The men were in good spirits. Somehow the word had spread that Major General William Farrar Smith's Eighteenth Corps was on ahead, and that the Sixth Corps was preparing to follow the Ninth. No one knew anything about Gouverneur Warren's Fifth Corps, or Hancock's Second Corps. There was something very mysterious and exhilarating about the whole thing. Amid the stealthy, muffled thud of boots in the ranks of the 48th Pennsylvania Volunteers, a sergeant whispered to Pleasants.

"You know where we're goin', Colonel?"

"We're going where they tell us to go," Pleasants muttered. "Just keep quiet and keep moving."

During the night, the Eighteenth Corps turned off at a

crossroads, its destination unknown. The Ninth peeled off along another route, directly south. In the wee hours of the night a rest halt was called, but shortly before daybreak the march was resumed.

Back in the area around Cold Harbor, Confederate patrols were beginning to puzzle over the strange stillness in the sector that had been so thickly populated by their enemies, and soon they would sally farther from their lines to investigate the situation, and report back their eerie, unbelievable discovery that the whole Army of the Potomac, to the last man, had been swallowed up during the night.

A few miles away, near White Oak Swamp—disconcertingly near the Rebel lines—other patrols were shortly to detect advance elements of Major General G. K. Warren's Fifth Corps, which had crossed the Chickahominy at midnight and now gave every indication of spearheading a drive toward Richmond. Not for several days would it be learned that this bold maneuver was a feint calculated to deceive, a smoke screen behind which the real objective of the Army of the Potomac was successfully hidden.

All day long Monday, the 13th, Burnside's Ninth Corps marched rapidly, with the Sixth Corps following. Late in the afternoon, advance details reached the bank of the James River, to find a battalion of engineers swarming over tremendous piles of material and hacking out an approach to a bridge not yet built. Early next day the main body of the Ninth Corps arrived at river's edge, and Lieutenant Colonel Pleasants, gazing across the expanse of waterway that he judged to be nearly a half mile wide, suddenly fitted together the jigsaw pieces in the puzzle of Grant's strategy, and smiled to himself.

Petersburg, of course! The "backdoor" tactics proposed by McClellan two years earlier in the Peninsular Campaign were at last to be tested. It was a gamble that might succeed. If Grant could get his troops over this river without

35

too much delay, if they could advance fast on Petersburg and strike hard, and, above all, if Lee could be prevented from shifting his lines south from Richmond, Petersburg could be taken, and the lifeline to the Confederate capital severed. They were three big if's, and not the least of them was the first. If Grant could get his army over the river . . .

Incredibly, a miracle took place. At four o'clock in the afternoon, engineers began working from opposite shores. Three schooners appeared and were maneuvered into position in midstream, then moored to serve as main supports for the span. A string of more than a hundred pontoons and a number of rafts were stretched across the water. Foot by foot, yard by yard, the bridge planking was pushed forward and spiked down, and by midnight the ends of the planking met over the middle of the river. The shaky but substantial trestle had been completed in eight hours of sweaty, hazardous toil, and from a vantage point near the shore where he had watched the construction with a practiced eye, Pleasants could not restrain a subdued cheer.

Now the human log jam could begin the ponderous job of disentangling itself. Slowly, but with surprisingly little delay and in good order, the artillery trains of the Ninth Corps moved forward to the bridge approaches and began lumbering across the span. By this time General Warren's Fifth Corps had rejoined the main body of troops, and its artillery, followed by that of the Sixth Corps, fell in behind the Ninth. All night long the thudding hoofs of the horses and the rumble of heavy wheels echoed hollowly over the dark river. It was an awesome, sinister sound that Henry Pleasants would remember for the rest of his life.

Now the last of the guns had rolled onto the far shore, and an exasperating period of delay set in for the massed infantry poised to follow. The word went round: "Waiting for orders." And daylight came on that morning of Wednesday, June 15, and nothing happened.

In Petersburg, sixteen miles away, plenty was happening. Baldy Smith's mysteriously maneuvering Eighteenth Corps had silently moved up the James on transports only a few hours before Grant's engineers bridged the river. Their route from Cold Harbor had taken them to the Union base at White House, on the Pamunkey River, and thence down the Pamunkey to Fortress Monroe and up the James to Bermuda Hundred. Now they were crossing a pontoon bridge over the Appomattox near City Point, picking up an undersized division of Negro troops belonging to General Ben Butler's Army of the James, and preparing to march on Petersburg, eight miles straight ahead.

Not until that evening was Pleasants to know that the Eighteenth Corps had contacted the enemy. The news arrived simultaneously with an order from General Meade telling General Burnside to hustle his Ninth Corps over the river and push on with all possible speed to Petersburg. The attack was under way, and every last outfit clogging the roads and woods in the vast assembly area north of the James was going over the river to bolster the drive. The Fifth Corps would follow the Ninth. The Sixth Corps would hold the north bank area until every other unit had crossed, then it would bring up the rear. The Engineer Battalion would dismantle the bridge, and the whole Army of the Potomac would be straightened out from its flanking movement for a frontal smash on Petersburg.

During the Ninth Corps' forced march, scant details of what had taken place earlier that day were circulated. The Eighteenth Corps, with its auxiliary division of colored troops, had advanced under light-to-medium skirmishing to within striking distance of the main fortifications guarding Petersburg. General Smith had then called a halt to make a thorough reconnaissance, and he had been so deeply impressed by the apparent strength and solidity of the defenses ahead of him that he hesitated for a long time to mount the full-scale assault he had been ordered to make. Around seven o'clock that evening—several hours before Meade ordered the Army of the Potomac to get moving— Smith had finally put up an artillery barrage and pushed his force of better than 10,000 men forward. After ninety minutes of hammering at the sturdy redans and trenches of the Confederate line, he had captured a mile-and-a-half-long section of the outer works. Elated, he wired the news to the headquarters of the Army of the James, and it was relayed to Grant, who was equally elated, and who then touched off the order that swept the Army of the Potomac over the river.

All night long the Ninth and Fifth Corps slogged forward. Meanwhile, the Eighteenth Corps had been relieved by the arrival of Hancock's Second Corps. Early in the morning the latter had been ordered to advance in support of Smith, and was expected to catch up with the Eighteenth Corps in time to participate in the attack on the lines. But all that afternoon the Second Corps was engaged in trying to solve the riddle of an erroneous map. Late in the day, when Hancock had finally found the right road, he was apprised for the first time in messages from both Grant and Smith that a fight was going on at Petersburg and that he was to get his corps there as quickly as possible.

The fight was all over when Hancock's troops arrived after a hurried moonlight march. Conferring together, Hancock and Smith fell into immediate disagreement over the next move. The former was all for following up the advantage Smith had gained by pressing forward the attack in the hope of taking the city before Rebel reinforcements arrived. Smith disagreed, with the condescension of a man who has gained an objective on his own and therefore feels better qualified to judge the situation than a Johnny-come-lately. He decided to hold the captured position and wait until daylight.

History was to prove that the decision was a fatal one. For even while the two corps leaders argued, General Beauregard, in command of the Confederate lines at Bermuda Hundred, ten miles away, had gotten wind of the threat to Petersburg and was preparing to abandon his position in order to reinforce the city's garrison. This step Beauregard made literally on his own. He had wired to Lee his suspicions of a massive offensive by the Army of the Potomac. Lee had wired back that he simply did not know Grant's whereabouts. Completely outfoxed by the withdrawal of the Union army from his own sector, and by the feint of Warren's corps toward Richmond, he was totally in the dark as to what was going on—would remain in the dark for another forty-eight hours.

And so "Old Bory," on his own initiative, was bolstering the defense of Petersburg with troops from his own line at Bermuda Hundred. All through the night he poured men into the city, while the Second and Eighteenth Corps slept on their arms. When daylight came, June 16, more than 14,000 Confederate infantry filled the Petersburg entrenchments, and the momentous opportunity—to take the city by storm while its defenses were still thinly manned—was gone.

Morning brought reinforcements to the Federals, too. Weary from its all-night march, the Second Brigade of Ninth Corps' Second Division arrived on the scene and was placed in position to support an attack which Grant had ordered to be made later in the day. Hancock now had been placed in command of all the troops comprising the initial massed assault force, and Burnside's men, as fast as they arrived, were sent into line alongside Brigadier General Francis C. Barlow's division of the Second Corps, and two brigades of the Eighteenth Corps.

By six o'clock that evening the assault was under way. Union artillery had been posted in the captured fortifications, and heavy fire was concentrated on a new inner line of earthworks which the Rebels had feverishly thrown up during the night. Covered by the bombardment, Barlow's division and its supporting brigades from the Ninth and Eighteenth Corps advanced, but met with furious opposition from Beauregard's seasoned veterans in the trenches. The new fortifications were surprisingly strong, and they held. After an hour's struggle, General Hancock silenced his guns and retired the assault forces. Tomorrow was another day, and with more and more columns of the Army of the Potomac arriving hourly, there was no point in continuing to bruise one's knuckles against an impregnable wall for the sake of a minor time advantage.

Lieutenant Colonel Henry Pleasants and his 48th Pennsylvania Volunteers had come up, winded and worn, in time to witness the ineffectual attack, and were promptly formed in line of battle. Exhausted as they were by their rapid march, they welcomed the respite brought on by nightfall. As darkness deepened, and there appeared to be no immediate prospect of action, the men dozed fitfully on their arms. Pleasants, who had been busy reconnoitering the terrain between his position and the nearest enemy forts, remained alert for anticipated orders—and shortly after midnight they came.

The brigades of Brigadier General R. B. Potter's division were to make a surprise attack on the forts at dawn, and Pleasants was to get his regiment into position well before daylight. It was to be a bayonet assault; not a shot was to be fired. Tin cups, mess equipment, all other loose metal objects were to be made secure in knapsacks, so that not a rattle could be heard.

Pleasants assembled his men in the darkness, and passed the word along to his company commanders that the mission was a dangerous one, and that anyone who wished to remain behind had his permission to do so. Not a man accepted his offer. Bayonets were silently fixed, caps removed

40

from rifles lest a chance shot spoil the plan. Crossing a narrow creek that separated them from the forts, Pleasants' Pennsylvanians advanced slowly and silently for a hundred yards, threading their way through a formidable abatis of felled timbers. Halting almost in the shadow of the nearer of the two forts, they waited for the signal to attack.

Just as dawn began to tinge the eastern sky, the signal was given. Up the short incline went the 48th—"like rabbits, clawing at underbrush to keep our footing, until we felt the soft earth of the breastworks under our feet," Pleasants recalled later. With wild yells, the men vaulted over the ramparts, landing in the midst of the surprised enemy, roused from sleep. The defenders managed to fire a few shots, then quickly surrendered. A moment later, discovering that things had not gone quite so smoothly in the assault on the adjacent fort, Pleasants led his men in a wild attack that thoroughly routed the enemy from that position.

Virtually alone, the 48th Pennsylvania Volunteers had taken two strong redans, 600 prisoners, 1,500 arms, considerable ammunition, and four pieces of artillery, complete with caissons and horses. Only a few hours after arriving on the scene, they had carried their colors to the farthest point yet reached in the Petersburg offensive. It was a praiseworthy achievement.

Flushed with success, Pleasants withdrew to report to his brigade commander, Colonel Curtin, and was instructed to hold his advanced position in the lines. Back among his men, he gave orders to dig in. By daylight, under protecting artillery fire, he made desperate efforts to advance farther. Next day, June 18, he led the 48th on a last grim assault, and managed to drive the enemy back across a railroad gully. In this fierce action, carrying the weight of Potter's full division, Colonel Curtin was gravely wounded and was moved to the rear. A new brigade commander was needed immediately, and without hesitation Potter wrote

41

the order that placed Lieutenant Colonel Henry Pleasants in command.

It was a fleeting moment of triumph for the tight-lipped, hard-jawed young mining engineer turned soldier, a triumph that he could recount proudly in his next letter to Anne Shaw, in Lexington. Impulsively, his men cheered him when they heard the news. Now the situation was in hand. The 48th, from good old Schuylkill County, Pennsylvania, would show the rest of the Army of the Potomac how to take the spunk out of the Rebels. Petersburg was doomed to fall.

But the situation was not in hand. Quite suddenly, it was very much out of hand. And Petersburg, doomed though it was, was a prize still far out of reach at this moment. Frustrated, confused, uncoordinated, Grant's mighty military machine was slowing down to a standstill.

5

An Idea Is Born

Too much had happened in two weeks, and yet not enough. The Union forces had moved with surprising suddenness and speed, and they had struck hard. But there had been a compounding of minor delays, a few serious errors in judgment, and inexplicably poor timing in several instances. These added up as important factors in the human equation, and with them was included another consideration: the utter exhaustion of officers and men.

For six days in a row many of the troops had been almost constantly on the move. Some, like the Ninth Corps Second Brigade, had been hurried to the front by forced marches and flung into the attack virtually without respite. It was more than flesh and blood could stand. Aggravating the frightful strain was the heat. There had been no rain since Cold Harbor, and no prospect of any immediate relief from the developing dry spell. General Meade, watching the last desperate flurry of attacks against the Confederate positions in the late afternoon of June 18, matter-of-factly observed that a lot of the vigor had gone out of the Union drive.

Still another circumstance had occurred to explain that lack of vigor. General Robert E. Lee had at last comprehended the situation, and the seriousness of the threat to Petersburg, and was sending heavy reinforcements from

43

his army to shore up Beauregard's defense of the city. It was reported that Lee himself, and A. P. Hill, had arrived on the scene. Psychologically, this news plunged the Army of the Potomac into a slough of dejection.

No doubt Grant was the first to realize that an impasse had been reached, and he faced it in his typically phlegmatic manner. It was not in his nature to berate or chide those who, with good intent, had contributed to the sum total of mistakes that had produced this stalemate. Time and the weight of numbers were on his side, and if Petersburg could not be taken quickly it would be taken slowly. Thus on Saturday night, June 18, he conferred with Meade on the advisability of resting the troops under cover, relocating his artillery, bringing up and entrenching all available reinforcements, and settling down to a long siege.

The campaign of the Union forces at this time is perhaps less understood and appreciated than most of the major operations of the War Between the States. To a considerable degree this is so simply because a defeated army seldom is accorded the same credit, in proportion to whatever its achievements may have been, that a victorious army receives. At the close of this war, popular interest centered naturally on those operations which most dramatically reflected credit on the records of the Northern generals. Only in comparatively recent years has there been any pronounced tendency on the part of historians to analyze tactical procedures in the light of complete impartiality. Often, when such analyses are attempted, the findings prove unpopular—for in such cases heroes sometimes emerge as less than heroes, victories frequently are devaluated, and losers are shown to be deserving of more merit than had been accorded them. And because such evidence runs counter to the human concept of orderly human endeavor, humans are generally reluctant to accept it.

General Ulysses S. Grant had been chosen for leadership

because of the qualities he had exhibited so successfully in the siege of Vicksburg, Mississippi, the previous July. They were safe qualities, resulting in the gaining of objectives by careful planning, deliberation, and tenacity, rather than by any spectacular feats of boldness. He was not considered brilliant by many of his associates, least of all by those of the Regular Army over whose heads he had been promoted, but President Lincoln had great confidence in the crushing, grinding methods by which this impassive man achieved his purposes. "He wins battles," was an effective riposte to the critics—although there were those who countered with, "He loses men." He had lost upward of 10,000 between June 15 and 18.

Yet Lincoln's confidence was not misplaced. Grant's dogged persistence, his determination to overcome fanatical bravery and skilled leadership by sheer force of numbers in a comprehensive but slow-moving campaign, were finally justified. Petersburg eventually was taken—but only on the third of April, 1865, just nine months and sixteen days after Colonel Pleasants and the 48th Pennsylvania Volunteers made their memorable night attack on the fort and redan, and established a salient in the Union lines at the point nearest the Confederate defenses and the city itself.

In this month of June, 1864, however, the day of capitulation was still a long way off, and by the time it arrived the cost of the campaign would be unbelievably great. Nevertheless, there was no apparent alternative. Grant had ordered the siege, and he was preparing to stick it out for as long as necessary. He was a patient man, not easily depressed by costs. He would slowly strangle Petersburg with his right hand, and with his left he would unceasingly harass the pipe lines of Rebel supply—the railroads that fanned out to the south and west of the city.

By June 20 the Union line was firmly established. It extended from a point near the Appomattox River, east of the

45

city, to the Ninth Corps salient which remained in closest proximity to the enemy lines, then ran irregularly southward and westward at an increasingly greater distance from the city. Opposite the salient, behind the Confederate lines, lay Blandford Cemetery, situated on a commanding elevation of ground beyond which the church spires of Petersburg were clearly outlined against the sky. This elevation, referred to on Union maps as Cemetery Hill, was a key point in the city's defenses, and a position greatly coveted by the Army of the Potomac for its tactical advantages. But Confederate fortifications at this point were particularly impregnable because of the strategic location of a solidly constructed earth fort on a steep slope halfway between the salient and Cemetery Hill. All assaults against this fort had failed, and it was only after he had weighed and discounted the advisability of any further attempts to capture it that Grant resigned himself to the siege.

Trench warfare, at best, is extremely trying, and Grant's soldiers took to it no better than the soldiers of any other military campaign in history. Once they had gained their sorely needed rest they were bored by inactivity, irritated by physical discomforts, occasionally unnerved by the devilish accuracy of Confederate sharpshooters. Summer had come on, and the blazing heat in the entrenchments was almost unbearable. Sanitary conditions were bad, and the water supply from a small creek that flowed through the Union lines had become polluted. The situation, far worse for the besiegers than for the besieged, gave no promise of improving.

By June 23, three days after the establishment of the Union lines, Colonel Pleasants began to feel the effects of the inaction. Although now commanding the First Brigade, he spent considerable time with the officers and men of the 48th Pennsylvania Regiment, who knew only too well the signs of his restless, nervous temperament. Captain Joseph

H. Hoskings, who was made commander of Company C when Pleasants became regimental commander, had been moved up to replace him as the leader of the 48th. The two were old friends, and Hoskings felt keenly the alternating moods of fretfulness and despondency that betrayed Pleasants' unhappy state of mind.

Small annoyances became monstrous. Every time one of his men was winged by a sharpshooter, Pleasants shook his fist in rage toward the enemy. He found fault with the entrenchments, insisting that they be dug deeper, and the breastworks made more solid. He berated the men who heedlessly exposed themselves and ordered them to take cover. He hovered over the cooks, complained to the commissary when supplies were inadequate. He was, in short, a man very much out of sorts, bristling with impatience, and outspokenly critical of the tactical policies adopted. A dozen times a day, as he made the rounds of his brigade, he looked across the fields to the wooded rise of Cemetery Hill. Each time, his eyes came back to the impregnable fort that guarded it.

From prisoners and other sources of information it had been learned that this fort was manned by a battery under General John Pegram, and that the troops supporting it were the best of the Rebel infantry. The battery was in excellent position to enfilade any attacking forces from the east and west, and any direct assault upon it would be foolhardy, since the ground in front of the fort ran all the way down to the Ninth Corps salient in a steep slope, completely devoid of cover.

"If we could only knock out that fort, the rest would be easy," Pleasants told Hoskings.

"Sure," agreed Hoskings. "But how can we do it?"

The question was academic, unanswerable. Yet within twenty-four hours an answer came—from a totally unexpected source.

47

It was the following evening, June 23, that Pleasants stood on a little rise of ground behind the line of his old regiment, again looking out over the terrain that stretched steeply upward to Cemetery Hill. Near by, two enlisted men from C Company were sharing the view and talking in low tones. Suddenly, in a voice that fell on Pleasants' ear softly but with beautiful clarity, one of them said:

"We could blow that damned fort out of existence if we could run a mine shaft under it."

History has not recorded the name of the man who gave utterance to the idea. Whoever it was, it is quite possible that his remark was an expression of wishful thinking, rather than a statement distilled through any process of reasoning. Perhaps he merely voiced an observation that sprang up automatically, as a sort of reflex impulse, from his peacetime occupational background. In any case, the seed fell on fertile soil.

Pleasants walked slowly back to his tent among the trees on the opposite side of the old railroad cut, through which his troops had driven the enemy at the time of the first attack. Captain George W. Gowen, now commanding Company C, was sitting on a box by the foot of his cot, trying to read by the flickering light of a candle. He arose and saluted, although he was one of Colonel Pleasants' warmest personal friends. Regimental and brigade courtesies were rigidly observed. Pleasants returned the salute, then threw off his coat and stretched his muscular arms to the ridgepole.

"Gowen," he said slowly, "that fort up there on the slope is the only thing between us and Petersburg. I have an idea we can blow it up. I just heard one of the men in your company talking about it and it set me thinking."

His junior officer stared at him in astonishment for a moment. Suddenly, his eyes opened wide as he took in the feasibility of such a seemingly preposterous plan. "That's a wonderful idea, Pleasants. But look what a distance there is between the lines! So far as I know, nothing of that kind has ever been done before."

"What of it?" Pleasants countered. "The men in your company earned their daily bread, before the war, doing that very thing. I know, because I personally recruited most of them."

"But it is several hundred feet from our lines to the fort, at the closest point," Gowen objected. "Still"—he squinted his eyes in concentration—"it might be done. If you work out a plan, we'll tackle it."

Pleasants put on his coat, buckled on his side arms, and went off to see another old friend in the Eighteenth Corps, located some distance to the right of the Ninth Corps salient. Captain Frank Farquhar was Chief Engineer of the Eighteenth Corps, and a Pottsville man. He had been a civil engineer, with practical experience in anthracite mining projects and a background of excellent technical training. It would be wise, Pleasants felt, to get Farquhar's reaction before conveying his idea to higher-echelon officers.

Farquhar received him most cordially. They talked together for an hour or two, and Pleasants returned to his tent vastly encouraged, his mind filled with plans. Far into the night he lay awake on his cot, and the longer his brain grappled with the idea, the more firmly convinced he became that the fantastic project might succeed—might even prove to be the knockout punch that would end the war.

He was up next morning at daybreak, and threaded his way to the point nearest the Confederate lines to scan the slope toward the fort. His next move was to interview every company commander in the 48th Regiment and request him to furnish a list of all experienced coal miners in his unit. That evening he went to the headquarters of Brigadier General Robert B. Potter, commanding the Second Division of the Ninth Corps, and laid the whole matter before him.

Potter was a fine-looking man, with intelligent, thoughtful, almost sad eyes, a short cropped mustache, and sparse muttonchop whiskers that reminded one strongly of General Burnside. In fact, he was a great deal like Burnside in his heartiness and sincerity, as contrasted with the cold, punctilious formality of most of the higher officers, with the possible exception of General Grant. Potter listened to Pleasants with a keen interest and undivided attention that were gratifying. He then sent for Captain David McKibben of his staff, and the three of them talked for some time. While not fully committing himself, General Potter appeared to be favorably impressed with the plan. He directed McKibben to look over the ground with Colonel Pleasants the following day.

McKibben reported next morning, and Pleasants led the way to the advance trenches, getting as close to the Confederate line as possible. Raising his head cautiously over the earthworks, McKibben pointed out to his companion the exact location of the Rebel battery under which the shaft should be run. This was a most important point, and Pleasants started to jot down a note or two on a dispatch sheet, when suddenly he heard a loud "snap," like a man snapping his fingers. McKibben shuddered and reeled against him, the blood spurting out of a terrible wound in his face. He had been so intent on his observations that an enemy sharpshooter had spied him and had scored a direct hit.

Pleasants felt sick all over, for even his long exposure to the horrors of war had left him incapable of restraining an involuntary shudder whenever a man was struck. McKibben was a particularly brave, quiet, and unostentatious officer. He was completely conscious and, in spite of his injury, insisted on walking with Pleasants' support to the rear, where he was immediately removed to the hospital.

Fortunately, he recovered, later to be brevetted Brigadier General for gallantry in action.

McKibben had given the exact information Pleasants wanted most. He now saw that directly east of the fort, behind the Union lines, ran a deep gully lined with trees. This depression extended down into the main ravine, where the old railroad line had run. It would be possible for the mining troops to start operations behind the Union entrenchments at the head of this gully. In his tent, he drew a rough sketch of the terrain and the relative positions of the opposing troops. This he presented to General Potter, along with a résumé of the plan and the more important details involved in executing it. Potter promised to forward the material, and a personal report, to General Burnside immediately.

"Do you anticipate any delay in his reply, sir?" Pleasants asked anxiously.

"I anticipate nothing in this war, Colonel Pleasants," Potter answered kindly. "But I understand your impatience, and we shall hope for the best."

His friendly nod of dismissal conveyed the minimum of encouragement, although perhaps it was as much blessing as any man could ask in a venture so seemingly preposterous.

6

Red Tape War

The word got around, as it was bound to do, and its effect upon the enlisted men of the First Brigade was salutary to say the least. Especially to the personnel of the 48th Pennsylvania Regiment the news was almost galvanic, dispersing an apathy that had fastened itself upon them almost from the beginning of the siege. More than that, it rejuvenated their spirits and bolstered their sagging pride. A mine was to be laid under the enemy's key fortification, and they had been selected, above all other troops in the Army of the Potomac, to do the job. No one seemed to know exactly how that job was to be done, but the heads of the lads from Schuylkill County, Pennsylvania, seethed with conjecture. Morale, which had been going down steadily in the past ten days, climbed up again.

In Company C the veteran enlistees were especially elated and understandably proud. "If Pleasants is going to run this show, you can bet your boots it'll be run right," they boasted to the newer replacements. "He's our old C.O., and he was a hell of a good mining man, back in Pottsville."

Colonel Pleasants noted the undercurrent of change with satisfaction and accepted it as a good omen. He was less satisfied with his own feelings, which varied from enthusiasm to excitement, from deep-seated concern over the stag-

gering labors ahead to apprehension that some unforeseen obstruction might snag the plan before it could be carried out. And constantly there was the irritation of being obliged to proceed routinely through military channels, and of submitting to the maddening delays occasioned solely by protocol and formality.

He himself had absolute confidence in the practicability of the plan he had outlined. Naturally, this confidence was by no means shaken by the enthusiastic discussions he overheard daily among the men during his rounds of brigade inspection. He understood that these men now had an objective—that the blistering heat, lack of water, enemy sharpshooter fire, and other discomforts of trench warfare were reduced to minor annoyances. He was more proud of these men than ever. But now, as never before, he must control his own emotions. Above all, he must set an example of adherence to military procedure, however irksome it might become.

Despite this commendable resolve, he could not remain idle. When, twenty-four hours after calling on General Potter, no word had been received, he quietly assembled those men of the 48th who had been singled out because of their mining experience, and explained his general plan to them. He went even further. He organized these men into small details, showed them how to use their bayonets as picks, and set them to work burrowing like gophers under the camouflage of bushes at the head of the gully where he purposed to start his tunnel. As it was of the utmost importance that no fresh earth be observed by the enemy, he instructed the men to nail handles onto empty cracker boxes, and by this means carry each load of dirt down to the creek that ran near by. Any Rebel observers who chanced to notice this activity would assume that the creek was being dammed for washing clothes and bathing. And Pleasants complacently figured that any Union top brass looking in that direction would assume exactly the same thing. Thus the project was begun, June 25, on Pleasants' own initiative, secretly and without any official knowledge or sanction.

Next day, late in the afternoon, an aide arrived from General Potter. Potter sent his respects to Lieutenant Colonel Pleasants, and desired to see him immediately. In his division headquarters tent, the handsome man of the sad eyes and neat mustache returned Pleasants' salute casually but with correctness, and motioned him to a camp chair.

"I assured you, Colonel Pleasants, that I would communicate with General Burnside immediately in regard to your plan," Potter said. "I have done so, and I wanted you to see this copy of my message."

He extended a dispatch sheet covered with fine flowing script. Dated June 24, it had been channeled through Major General John G. Parks, Chief of Staff of the Ninth Army Corps, to General Burnside. Pleasants read every word carefully:

"General:—Lieutenant Colonel Henry Pleasants, of the Forty-Eighth Penna. Veteran Volunteers, commanding First Brigade, has called upon me to express his opinion of the feasibility of mining the enemy's works in my front. Colonel Pleasants was a mining engineer in charge of some of the principal works of Schuylkill County, Penna. He has in his command upwards of eighty-five enlisted men, and fourteen commissioned officers who are professional miners. The distance from inside our work, where the mine would have to be started, to the inside of the enemy's work, does not exceed one hundred yards. He is of the opinion that they could run a mine forward at the rate of twenty-five to fifty feet per day, including supports, ventilation, and so on. A few miners' picks, which I am informed could be made by any blacksmith from the

Colonel Henry Pleasants, Originator and Engineer of
the Mine at Petersburg, Va., June 1, 1864

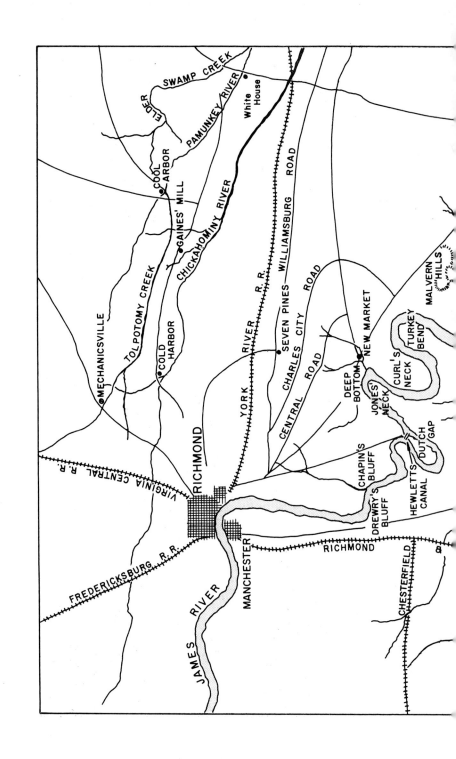

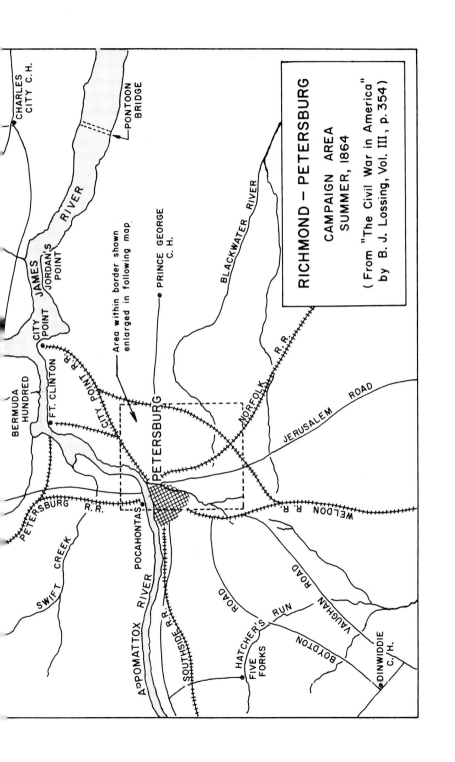

RICHMOND – PETERSBURG

CAMPAIGN AREA
SUMMER, 1864

(From "The Civil War in America"
by B. J. Lossing, Vol. III, p. 354)

CHARLES CITY C. H.

PONTOON BRIDGE

JAMES RIVER

JORDAN'S POINT

CITY POINT

Area within border shown
enlarged in following map.

PRINCE GEORGE C. H.

BLACKWATER RIVER

BERMUDA HUNDRED

FT. CLINTON

CITY POINT R. R.

NORFOLK R. R.

JERUSALEM ROAD

PETERSBURG

PETERSBURG R. R.

SWIFT CREEK

POCAHONTAS

APPOMATTOX RIVER

SOUTHSIDE R.R.

WELDON R. R.

HATCHER'S RUN

FIVE FORKS

ROAD

VAUGHAN ROAD

BOYDTON

DINWIDDIE C. H.

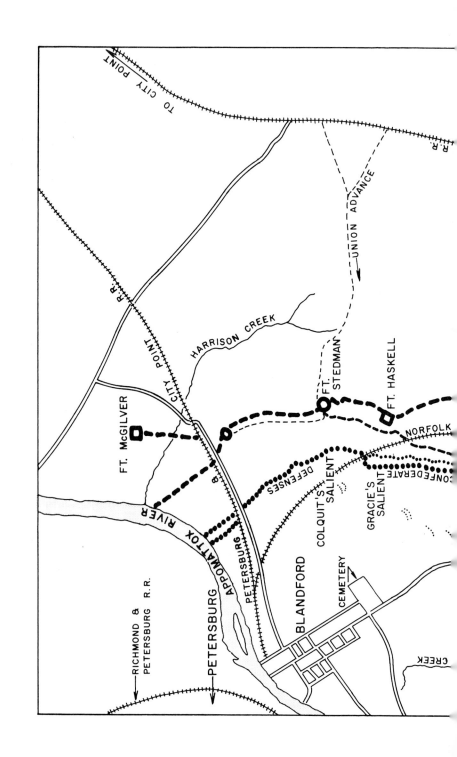

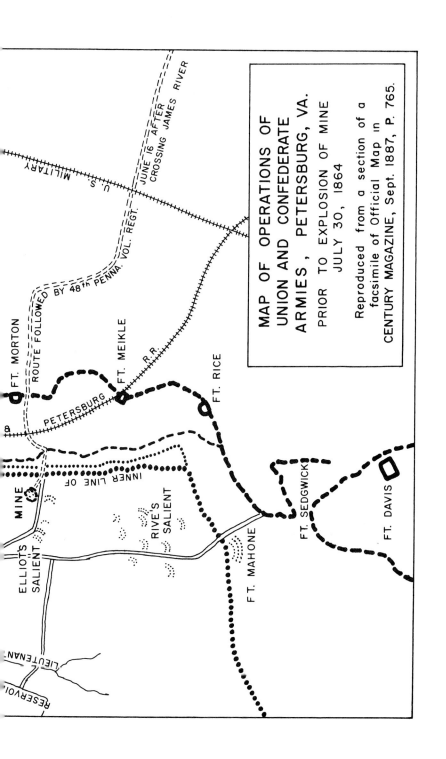

MAP OF OPERATIONS OF
UNION AND CONFEDERATE
ARMIES, PETERSBURG, VA.

PRIOR TO EXPLOSION OF MINE
JULY 30, 1864

Reproduced from a section of a
facsimile of Official Map in
CENTURY MAGAZINE, Sept. 1887, P. 765.

JUNE 16 AFTER
CROSSING JAMES RIVER

U.S. MILITARY

ROUTE FOLLOWED BY 48TH PENNA. VOL. REGT.

FT. MORTON

FT. MEIKLE

R.R.

PETERSBURG

FT. RICE

MINE

FT. SEDGWICK

FT. DAVIS

INNER LINE OF

RIVE'S SALIENT

ELLIOT'S SALIENT

FT. MAHONE

LIEUTENAN

RESERVOI

PETERSBURG, VA., LOOKING TOWARD RESERVOIR HILL.
ENTRANCE TO MINE IN RAVINE

RECONSTRUCTED ENTRANCE TO THE MINE

THE CRATER IMMEDIATELY AFTER THE ASSAULT

THE CRATER OCCUPIED BY CONFEDERATES AFTER THE ASSAULT

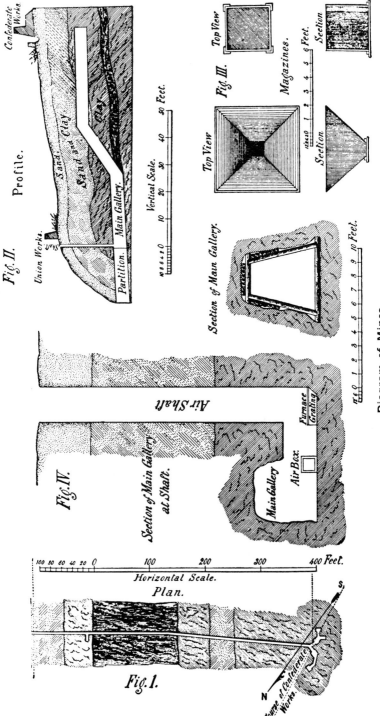

Fig. II.

Profile.

Confederate Works.

Sand and Clay.

Union Works.

Fig. I.

Main Gallery.

Partition.

Vertical Scale.

50   40   30   20   10   0
10 8 6 4 2 0   50 Feet.

Fig. III.

Top View

Magazines.

Section

1 2 3 4 5 6 Feet.
6 5 4 3 2 1 0

Top View

Section

Section

Section of Main Gallery.

1 2 3 4 5 6 7 8 9 10 Feet.
10 9 8 7 6 5 4 3 2 1 0

Diagram of Mines

Fig. IV.

Air Shaft

Section of Main Gallery at Shaft.

Main Gallery

Air Box.

Furnace
Grating

Plan.

Horizontal Scale.

100 80 60 40 20   0   100   200   300   400 Feet.

Fig. 1.

N

S

Course of Confederate Works.

ordinary ones; a few hand-barrows, easily constructed; one or two mathematical instruments, which would be supplied by the engineer department, and the ordinary entrenching tools, are all that are required. The men themselves have been talking about it, and are quite desirous, seemingly, of trying it. If you desire to see Col. Pleasants, I will ride over with him or send him up to you.

R. B. Potter, Brig. Genl."

"You have presented the case very clearly, sir," Pleasants said, "and I am grateful to you." He returned the paper to his superior officer, then wiped his brow with the back of his hand. "I had only hoped that, by this time, we might have a reply."

"We have," Potter smiled. "Less than thirty minutes ago a note arrived from General Burnside. I sent for you right away. He wants us to submit a detailed plan in writing, or else call upon him this evening. I imagine you would prefer the latter course."

"By all means, sir." Pleasants jumped to his feet. "That's wonderful news. I'll be ready whenever you are. I have a feeling, sir, that we can convince General Burnside of the feasibility of what we are doing—that is, of what we *propose* to do."

"Don't be too sure," Potter said gravely. "But we shall see."

Together they rode over to Burnside's tent at dusk. It was the first time that Pleasants had had an opportunity to talk with the Corps Commander, although he had met him occasionally in an official capacity. He was sitting in his tent with his coat off, his bald head shining in the flickering candlelight, a long cigar jutting at an angle from one corner of his mouth. Beads of sweat stood out on his forehead, and he wiped them off with a big silk bandanna as he rose to greet them. Colonel Pleasants felt instantly at ease, sure that he would have a sympathetic hearing, for there was a happy absence of the glassy eyed formality and cold punctilio so frequently encountered in conferences with higher-bracket Regular Army officers.

General Potter explained briefly the details of the plan of the mine. Burnside listened attentively, nodding his bald head and fingering his thick side whiskers while his eyes bored steadily into Potter's face. Clearly not a single detail was escaping him. When his divisional commander had finished he said quietly:

"General Potter, so far as I know, in all the history of warfare, no shaft or sap anywhere near the length of this one you propose has ever been attempted."

"That is true, General Burnside," Potter replied, "but Colonel Pleasants is an experienced mining engineer, and he is convinced that the idea is feasible. It seems reasonable to suppose that if shafts of this kind can be run in coal regions, they can be run here. And it seems worth while to make the attempt, for that fort is the only obstruction between our army and Petersburg. With it destroyed, a quick assault would carry Cemetery Hill, which commands the city. Speed is the important thing right now, for the Confederates are strengthening their positions daily, and reinforcements are coming in steadily. Besides that, our men are chafing from inaction. Since this mining project was first mentioned, the whole Division has had a tremendous uplift in morale. It would be wonderful if we could really capitalize on it at this critical time."

"Potter, I realize fully the truth of what you say," agreed Burnside. "Lee is concentrating all of his forces here, and a long siege will be costly for both sides. We are bound to win out in the end by sheer force of numbers, but I am very anxious to see the war end quickly." He began wiping his face nervously with the silk bandanna, and when he had finished, the candlelight reflected a new gleam in his eyes. He puffed slowly on his cigar for a minute or two as he stared out of the tent into the darkness. Presently, he said:

"Well, gentlemen, I am heartily in favor of the plan. You realize, however, that the authority for such operations, and for the troop movements, which are also to be considered, must come from the Commanding General of the Army of the Potomac, General George Gordon Meade. I will let you know his decision. You may not realize this, gentlemen, but I stand in a decidedly delicate position in relation to my superiors of the Regular Army. You must know very well that after our Ninth Corps had taken that bridge over Antietam Creek, and had routed the Confederates from the heights beyond, all we needed to crush Lee's army, and possibly end the war, were reinforcements and more ammunition. McClellan absolutely refused to give me that support. Consequently, the opportunity of a lifetime was lost. Now, in this project we must depend upon the support of Meade and his staff. Are we going to get it at the critical time?"

It was a question no one could answer, and it produced an awkward moment of silence. A moth flew into the tent, circled around the candle flame, and alighted on Burnside's knee. He destroyed it with a resounding slap. Turning to Pleasants, he said: "You think we'll smash 'em like that, eh?"

"I do, sir," said Pleasants, smiling.

"You really think you can do this thing? We're not mining coal, you know."

"I know. I'm sure we can do it."

"Good." Burnside stood up. "You have my authority to proceed. After all, there is no harm in going ahead, and the work can be suspended if it is not approved. But you will, of course, keep me informed of your progress. Remember, everything must be done through the proper channels, officially." He acknowledged their salutes, then shook hands with both officers. "Good night, gentlemen—and good luck."

Potter and Pleasants returned to Division Headquarters, well pleased with the conference. What had been obtained was a provisional endorsement of the plan by the Commanding General of the Ninth Corps, and his tentative permission to put the plan into operation. The forthright Burnside had thus far gone out on a limb. Now he would communicate with General Meade, who might, or might not, communicate with General Grant, and what the result would be was beyond conjecture. Burnside had betrayed his bitter awareness of the unwillingness of certain Union generals to cooperate with him. Obviously he was worried over the possibility that the plan outlined by Colonel Pleasants might meet with summary rejection, or, at best, a harshly circumscribed assent that would place full responsibility on his shoulders, and perhaps subject him to reprimand or ridicule if the project failed.

Lying awake on his cot that night, Pleasants felt both pride and sympathy for Burnside—pride in the Corps Commander's spunk and resolution, sympathy for his position of vulnerability to criticism. But perhaps there would be no occasion for criticism. The plan would be successful; it *must* be successful. And by hastening the project with all possible speed and efficiency, the work might very well reach a point of near-completion before either official approval or disapproval had filtered down through the chain of command.

Next morning, before sunup, Colonel Pleasants sought out Lieutenant Jacob Douty and Sergeant Henry Reese, his two closest associates in the 48th Regiment, and told them the news.

"General Burnside has given us his blessing and told us to start digging."

"We're pretty well started, sir," Douty said, grinning.

58

"And we're going to push right ahead. What have you figured can be done about timbers?"

"I don't know yet, sir. I understand there's an old bridge over a railroad track somewhere south of here, and if it's not too far, we might get some planks out of that. I thought I'd send a detail—"

"Never mind. I'll take a look myself."

Several days passed, and no word came from General Meade. Work on the tunnel progressed rapidly, however, and with so much enthusiasm on the part of the men selected for the digging that Pleasants had no difficulty maintaining full shifts around the clock. He had far more difficulty with the problem of obtaining timbers for the walls and roof of the tunnel as it lengthened. Five or six miles to the rear of the southeastern perimeter of Union fortifications there was a damaged bridge that spanned the tracks of the Norfolk and Petersburg Railroad at a point where they ran through a deep ravine. Pleasants personally reconnoitered the area, despite the risk of prowling enemy patrols, and he estimated that a large quantity of planking could be removed from the bridge without much difficulty. The problem was how to transport the heavy planks all the way back to the tunnel.

Pleasants went to Potter and explained the situation. Potter pointed out that artillery teams and wagons were available. "But the mission would be dangerous, sir," Pleasants said. "The men and the teams would require extra protection. My suggestion is that a troop of cavalry be requisitioned and assigned as an escort."

General Potter raised an eyebrow but immediately dashed off a dispatch to General Burnside. Burnside stroked his whiskers, hesitated only briefly, and forwarded the request to General Meade. There the communication came to a dead end, for Meade made no response. Desperate,

59

Pleasants finally sent two companies of his own men, with wagons, and managed to salvage a considerable amount of timber from the old bridge.

Later, when a new source of lumber had to be found, a scavenging detail located an abandoned sawmill, with several big stacks of pine boards stored in a shed on the premises. It was a better find than a diamond mine, but here too there was a grave risk; the place was far outside the Union lines, in enemy territory. Again, gritting his teeth in anxiety over the chance that some untoward incident might betray his whole project to the Rebels, Pleasants sent men and wagons to fetch the timber, and sighed with relief when the expedition triumphantly returned without having encountered any patrols.

Another problem of increasing concern was the removal of dirt from the steadily lengthening tunnel. From the commissary, Pleasants carried away all the empty cracker boxes he could lay hands on, to be used as barrows. These he girded stoutly with iron hoops removed from old pork and beef barrels, and to their sides he nailed long hickory handles. The boxes were big, and when they were filled with dirt and stone they were tremendously heavy. Sooner or later, all the boxes split open. Now and then a handle tore loose from the blistered grip of a sweating carrier. Hammer in fist, Pleasants made the repairs himself.

And somehow the work went on, despite the lack of top-rank sanction, despite the absence of proper tools and equipment. No special mining picks were available, but Pleasants had taken the regulation army picks to a smith who straightened them into push picks. Nothing was quite right, and nearly everything was wrong, and there was too much work and hardly enough of anything else. And the heat kept getting worse.

On the sixth day of July, Pleasants received a letter. He had just finished extracting a long splinter of wood from the hand of one of his miners, and now he dashed the sweat from his eyes to read a message marked "Headquarters, Army of the United States, City Point, Va." It was from the Chief of Army Engineers, under date of July 3. Delayed through channels, Pleasants told himself grimly—and then, as he unfolded the letter and squinted against the glare of the sun, the words buzzed from the page like a cloud of tormenting insects.

"Lieut. Col. Pleasants:—In order to be enabled to have a clear judgment of the progress of the mining work in front of General Burnside's rifle pits, I would like to be furnished with:

First, A rough longitudinal section made after a certain scale through our works, neighboring the mine, through the mine gallery, and through the enemy's works to be attacked by the mine. This section with all important numbers inscribed, will show, besides profiles of the mine gallery entrance with reference to our own defense line, the arrangement of the entrance, whether by shaft or by an inclined gallery, etc., the height of the gallery in both places not framed and such as are supplied with frames, the natural horizon near the entrance and near the powder chamber, and finally the location, length and height of the latter.

Second, A profile of the gallery showing its width in framed and unframed places and the width of the powder chamber.

Third (a) When was the mining work begun? (State day and hour.) (b) Has it been continued night and day without any interruption, and how many men were and are engaged on it at the same time? (c) When will the gallery be finished?

Fourth, What kind of soil is probably to be expected around the powder chamber?

Fifth, What is the intended weight of the charge, and what is the expected diameter of the crater measured on its surface?

Sixth, By what means shall the mine be fired, supposed that it shall be fired as soon as possible and with the least loss of time?

Seventh, What means shall be used for tamping the mine, and what length shall this be done?

Eighth, Where shall the standpoint be of the miner firing the charge?

Ninth, At what time in the day shall the mine be fired?

Tenth, What measures are premeditated by the engineer department in accordance with the Commanding General to secure the possession of the crater effected by the mine and to facilitate its defense?

The questions should be answered without delay and as shortly as possible, only with reference to its numbers, i.e., answers to the 3rd, a, b, c, &c.

J. G. Barnard, Brig. Gen., Chief of Eng.
U. S. Armies in the Field"

So this was the way things were done in the Army of the Potomac! Half angry, half amused, Pleasants reread the dispatch, resisting an impulse to rip the paper to pieces and toss the pieces over his shoulder. He thought of a line from Tom Paine: "These are the times that try men's souls. . . ." And then he remembered his promise to Burnside, that everything would be done through the proper channels, officially. He placed the letter in his pocket. That night, in the stifling heat of his tent, by candlelight, he penned an answer.

"Headquarters 48th. Penna. Vet. Vols.
Near Petersburg, Va., July 7, 1864
Brig. Gen. J. G. Barnard:—Answer to question 2nd:
The gallery or tunnel is supported by props along its

whole length, at a distance from each other ranging from three to thirty feet, according to the nature of the roof. When the tunnel reaches a point immediately underneath the enemy's breastworks, it is proposed to drive two galleries, each about one hundred feet in length, whose position will be immediately underneath the enemy's breastworks and fort.

Answer to question 3(a): At 12 P.M. on the 25th. of June 1864. (b) The mining has been carried on without interruption since it was begun. There are 210 men employed every 24 hours but only two can mine at a time at the extremities of the work. (c) The tunnel will reach the enemy's work in about seven or eight days.

Answer to question 4: Sandy soil.

Answer to questions 5, 6, 7, 8, 9, and 10: Still under consideration. The mine is ventilated by means of an air shaft, with a furnace to rarefy the air and boxes to carry the gases from the interior of the gallery to the shaft.

> Henry Pleasants, Lieut. Col.
> 48th Pa. Regt."

7

A Matter of Ventilation

At the headquarters of the Army of the Potomac at City Point, three miles from the Ninth Corps salient, General George Gordon Meade reread with mild scorn the communication from General Ambrose E. Burnside regarding the plan to mine the enemy fortifications. Burnside had made it plain that he personally favored the project, that he had given it tentative sanction which headquarters was free to revoke, but that he was now asking for top-rank endorsement. Meade would have to think about that.

The feeling of contempt which had been his first reaction deepened. This Lieutenant Colonel Pleasants, whoever he might be, was undoubtedly a glory seeker, filled with delusions of bizarre conquest that probably were brought on by the heat! Somehow he had managed to gain an audience with Burnside and infect the Corps Commander with his silly ideas. It was not surprising, thought Meade. Burnside was gullible, visionary, forever dreaming of a quick way to end the war.

And yet, it was perhaps best not to dismiss the matter too summarily. Only a day ago, Grant had expressed his willingness to explore whatever means might suggest themselves as practicable for putting more pressure on the enemy. This idea of Burnside's hardly seemed to fill the bill, but Grant might think differently. At any rate, there was perhaps some merit in letting a portion of the troops occupy their minds and energies in digging a tunnel. If the operation served no other purpose, it would at least keep the men busy, alert, and in good physical condition.

In time to come, Meade would have an opportunity to explain his reaction and response to Burnside's dispatch. He would say, for the official record, that "when the subject was brought to my knowledge, I authorized the continuance of the operations, sanctioned them, and trusted that the work would at some time result in forming an important part in our operations." Significantly, he would add: "But from the first I never considered that the location of General Burnside's mine was a proper one, because, from what I could ascertain, the position of the enemy's works and lines erected at that time, the position against which he operated, was not a suitable one in which to assault. . . ."

Thus by his own admission Meade took a very dim view of the mine project. What action he took to investigate the matter for himself, or to enlist the opinions of other high officers at headquarters, is much less clear. Certainly he did mention it to Grant, who immediately became preoccupied with the details of how the assault should be conducted after the mine was exploded, and apparently assumed no responsibility at all for the mine itself.

As a matter of fact, Grant was getting a little worried. His contemplated forays against the railroads to the south and west of Petersburg had been postponed, partly because of the terrible heat. Not a drop of rain had fallen since June 3. The whole countryside was appallingly parched. Powdery, suffocating dust covered the roads through the enemy's territory behind the Union lines. There was no surface water anywhere, and the troops had had to dig wells that were barely adequate for their needs. It was a bad time for troop movement, and so Grant had wisely decided to defer raiding the railroads. Meanwhile, was his grip on the beleaguered city as firm as he had supposed? Did he have the enemy treed, or was the enemy holding him at bay, keeping him pinned down and literally out of action? True, he had brought up a train of siege guns and heavy mortars, and shortly would be able to pound the Confederate works harder than his field artillery had been able to do, but he was anxious to make headway faster than the immediate circumstances promised would be possible.

Meade had also, perhaps at Grant's suggestion, brought Burnside's communication to the attention of General Barnard and Major James C. Duane, and, as has been shown, the former in due time concocted the precise inquiry into details which had proved so aggravating to Colonel Pleasants.

Major Duane, who was Chief Engineer of the Army of the Potomac, was at least as skeptical of the mine operation as Meade and Barnard. He was a competent engineer who had demonstrated his ability on a number of occasions —most recently in helping to construct the pontoon bridge across the James River. All the more stinging, then, was his dismissal of the mine project, as conveyed to Pleasants by General Burnside.

For eventually, and with genuine regret, Burnside had to tell Pleasants that no official word of approval had come from headquarters.

"I'm sorry, Colonel Pleasants," Burnside said, "but General Meade and Major Duane both say that this thing can't be done. They have told me it is all claptrap and nonsense —that such a length of mine has never been excavated in military operations, and could not possibly succeed. They are convinced that you will get the men smothered for lack of proper ventilation, or crushed by falling earth, or that the enemy will find out what is going on and thwart the plan entirely."

"Do they forbid us to continue work?" Pleasants asked quietly.

"That's the strange thing. They withhold their approval, yet they are not ordering us to stop." The Corps Commander sighed, and the sigh said plainly that there was nothing so strange about it, after all. It was, thought Pleasants, the old army game again. Burnside would be permitted to pull the chestnuts out of the fire, if he wished. If he succeeded, well and good; the dissenters would claim that they had not obstructed him, that they had only pointed out the hazards, and that they had given what help they could. If he failed, he alone could be most conspicuously singled out for blame.

But the mine, Pleasants told himself grimly for the hundreth time, must *not* fail.

"Do we go ahead then, sir?"

"We go ahead," Burnside said firmly.

So now the die was cast, and there was no longer any question of help from higher headquarters. Whatever materials were needed would have to come, as the timbers had come, from such sources as might be discovered at hand. Whatever tools and equipment were lacking would have to be improvised or dispensed with. A hell of a way to fight a war, thought Pleasants, although there was some small satisfaction in knowing how things stood.

More than once during the next several days he would recall bitterly what Burnside had said about Meade and Duane. He had not expected much from the Commanding General of the Army of the Potomac, but he was disappointed in the Chief Engineer. He remembered a book Duane had written some years before the war, as Captain of the Corps of Army Engineers. The book was *A Manual for Engineer Troops,* and it contained a section on practical operations in mining. Pleasants had been favorably impressed by the author's thoroughness, and could recall now some of the tools enumerated as essential for such operations. Duane had included, in addition to pickaxes, push picks, shovels and wheelbarrows, such items as boring rods, a ventilating tube and flexible joints, and a bellows. Where, Pleasants would have liked to ask Duane, do you get these articles when a hardheaded army commander and his equally hardheaded chief engineer are uncooperative?

It had been tough going, up to now. It would be tough going all the way. Resigned at last to the dismal fact that he was never to receive any assistance from Headquarters of the Army of the Potomac, Pleasants applied all the energy and ingenuity of which he was capable to solving the problems of the operation as fast as they arose. They arose in quick succession, and some of them were enormous. One in particular—the one that the big men at Headquarters had smugly prophesied could not be licked—presented itself early in the mine operation.

It was the matter of ventilation. Before the tunnel had penetrated to any considerable distance, it was imperative that steps be taken to protect the men from suffocating. Pleasants sent a message to Duane. Could the Chief Engineer procure a miner's bellows to be used in forcing fresh air into the excavation? Duane apparently could not. When General Potter learned of the predicament, he was concerned enough to send for Pleasants.

"What do you propose to do, Colonel?" he asked worriedly.

"I shall try to work something out, sir," Pleasants said. Abstractedly, he clenched his right fist, patted it softly into the palm of his left hand. His thoughts were miles away. "Did you ever hear of the Sand Patch Tunnel, sir?"

"No. A military operation?"

"A railroad construction job I once worked on. Excuse me, sir. I was just thinking. I may be able to come up with something."

"I hope you do, Colonel Pleasants," Potter said gravely.

The Sand Patch Tunnel! There was the answer to the problem. Pleasants had solved the riddle of ventilation at that time for the Pennsylvania Railroad. Perhaps the same solution would serve now. This situation, of course, was different. The mouth of the mine was nearly a hundred feet behind the most advanced entrenchments of the Ninth Corps salient. Beyond the salient, it was more than 400 feet to the enemy fort. Obviously, any air shafts dug to ventilate the mine would have to be sunk behind the salient, within a hundred feet of the mouth, yet would have to supply air to the entire length of the tunnel as it progressed. It might not work, but it was worth trying.

Back of the salient's most advanced point, but as far from the mouth of the tunnel as possible, Pleasants had his men sink a perpendicular shaft, two feet in diameter, straight down from the bottom of a near-by rifle pit. At the proper depth, the shaft was dug horizontally to connect with the tunnel. Next he made an airtight canvas door shutting off the section of the tunnel between the shaft and the mouth, and built a hot fire in a pit covered by a furnace grating at the bottom of the shaft. As the work progressed, he constructed a tight wooden duct that extended from outside the tunnel to the farthest point where the miners were digging. It worked like magic. The hot fire created a draft that drew the foul air from the tunnel and forced it up the shaft, while the vacuum thus created sucked in fresh air through the wooden duct. As the tunnel lengthened, new sections had to be added to the duct to lengthen it accordingly, and a roaring fire had to be kept going continuously in the furnace pit in order to maintain constant circulation of fresh air.

"I've worked out a scheme for the ventilation, and it's functioning perfectly, sir," Pleasants reported to General Potter, describing the method.

69

"Good!" Potter exclaimed. "I'm greatly relieved"—and he looked it. He passed the word on to General Burnside.

"Good!" echoed Burnside. "That colonel of yours is a damned clever young man, Potter."

Clever he was, and determined, too. A man had to be both, to contend with the trials and reverses that seemed to be spawned endlessly, one after another, in the dark gallery of the mine.

There was, for instance, the water seepage. It had become so serious at one point that the timbering of the tunnel walls and ceiling was accomplished only with great difficulty. Then, suddenly, the footings sank in the soft earth and the ceiling supports bowed in. Several of the miners narrowly escaped being crushed between the roof and the floor, and hours of precious time were used up in shoring the collapsed area with heavy posts, and retimbering.

Another problem arose when the sandy soil, through which the digging had been progressing rapidly, gave way to a stratum of marl. When the report of this obstruction reached Pleasants, he hurried into the tunnel, grasped a pick from one of the miners, and for ten minutes jabbed desperately at the puttylike substance. It yielded, but slowly. The job would take forever if the men had to hack their way through this stuff. So Pleasants had the miners knock off their labors, and while they sat idle, amusing themselves by fashioning souvenirs from gobs of the marl, he charted a new course of direction for the tunnel. To get past the stratum of marl, he specified a seven-degree incline that would carry the tunnel over this obstruction. This slowed progress for a while, but eventually the digging was resumed under much more favorable conditions.

Fortunately, in changing the incline of the tunnel, Pleasants had the use of a theodolite to make his calculations. Earlier, the matter of obtaining this fundamental engineering instrument had been a problem in itself. Naturally a mobile fighting unit was not equipped with a theodolite, but Pleasants happened to know that there was one at Meade's headquarters. Again he sent an urgent note to Major Duane, requesting the loan of it. The note was not acknowledged, and the instrument was not forthcoming. Worried, anxious, and resentful, Pleasants was forced to conclude that since both Meade and Duane had said that the running of the mine was not possible, they had not the slightest intention of letting one of Burnside's lowly brigade commanders prove them in error.

It was Burnside himself who came nobly to the rescue. Acting on his own initiative, he sent a telegram to an influential friend in Washington, and within a couple of days an old-fashioned theodolite was delivered to Pleasants.

"If that thing had been made out of solid gold, and set with diamonds, it could not have been more precious to me," he commented later in a letter to Anne Shaw.

Little by little, the memory of Anne, and of those happy days in Lexington with her, was gently effacing the more distant memory of the tragedy of Sallie. How far away it all seemed—as though all of his life had been lived in a war without beginning and without end, and everything that had gone before belonged to a time and an existence from which he had been reincarnated. The truth was there was scant opportunity to contemplate either the memory of Sallie, or the memory of Anne. All of his mind and energy were wrestling with the problems of the mine. He had become obsessed with the vision of a gigantic blast that would completely shatter the weakened foundations of the Confederacy, bring the South to her knees, and end the war on a single crescendo note of unanswerable violence.

Not all of the difficulties and dangers originated inside the tunnel. Some of them arose from without, such as the occasions when it was necessary for Colonel Pleasants to check his calculations of distance and direction to be sure that his miners were staying accurately on course. These calculations had to be made from the most advanced point of the Ninth Corps salient, the very spot on which he had stood when Captain McKibben was so desperately wounded at his side. The old-fashioned theodolite, with its shiny brass tube shrouded in burlap, had to be set up in the most advanced trench. Even with the utmost precaution and the use of all possible cover and concealment, the job was hazardous. Pleasants crouched low in the trench, waited motionless for a few minutes, then snatched the burlap cover from the theodolite and made a quick triangulation.

The first time he was able to do this, following the wounding of McKibben, he came so close to being a casualty himself that he decided to try a ruse on his next trip to the danger spot. Several days later, when it was imperative that another triangulation be made, he worked his way cautiously to the forward line and ordered half a dozen riflemen to congregate in the trench at a little distance from his vantage point, and raise his hat, together with theirs, on bayonets held just above the breastworks. This, he hoped, would create the illusion that an officer was discussing some important matter with his men, and that the group thus engaged had carelessly exposed their heads above cover.

The ruse worked perfectly. No sooner was the theodolite in place, and the bayonets raised, than the air was full of bullets. But knowing that the fire was not being directed at him, Pleasants straightened up boldly and made his calculations with deliberation. In all, before the mine was completed, five triangulations were made, and twice as many bullet holes decorated Pleasants' campaign hat.

As the month of July advanced, so did the work on the tunnel. Interest in the operation had spread widely among all the troops, and of the thousands entrenched around Petersburg there were many who wished that they might have a hand in it. However, only the men of the 48th Pennsylvania Regiment were engaged in the work, although as the tunnel grew longer and the need for help increased proportionately, almost every man in the regiment was pressed into service. These numbered about 400. They worked in two-and-a-half-hour shifts, each shift in the charge of two officers. At the completion of a shift the men coming off duty were given a ration of whiskey—small enough compensation, for all of the labors involved were now intensified, particularly the task of lugging the cracker-box barrows of soil and stone out through the long gallery of the mine.

The difficulty of disposing of the excavated material had also increased. As much as possible was dumped into the railroad gully directly behind the Ninth Corps salient, and covered with brush to conceal it from enemy observation. Other quantities were distributed in the bed of the creek that flowed thinly through the Union lines, and in as many other unobtrusive spots as could be found. Time and again, Pleasants was convinced that some phase of the operations had alerted the enemy to what was going on. Yet nothing that he could observe confirmed this. Day after day the artillery bombardment went on, at intervals, and troops in the forward trenches exchanged rifle shots. Much of this desultory action, though trying, was ineffectual and routine, with no variation to indicate that suspicion had been aroused.

But on Sunday, July 17, disturbing news reached Colonel Pleasants. It was late in the afternoon, and he had just reached the definite conclusion, based on a fifth and final triangulation, that the main gallery of the mine now extended as far as it had to go. If his calculations were correct, the point where his men were now digging should be

73

directly under the enemy fort. He therefore halted excavation on the main gallery, and directed the commencement of digging operations on two lateral galleries, extending to the right and left like the crossing of a capital T. And then word was relayed from observers in some of the forward rifle pits, to the effect that the Rebels had been seen engaging in some activity that suggested that they, too, might be digging a tunnel!

Instantly the glow of success on the grimy faces of Pleasants' miners vanished in lines of consternation. Was this to be the pay-off? Had the enemy known all along what was taking place, waited until the terminus of the tunnel was under their fort, and then started countermining? If so, they could cancel out in three hours all the toil, sweat, and scheming of three weeks.

Pleasants received the report with a sickening feeling of despair. This was what he had feared from the very beginning. He had employed every precaution to insure secrecy, had warned Lieutenant Douty, Sergeant Reese, and every officer and man in the 48th to exercise the greatest possible care in order not to betray the undertaking either by sound or movement. So far as he could learn, these orders had been strictly observed. It was incredible that the Confederates had found out in spite of all precautions. Perhaps, while the digging was going on directly beneath the fort, the muffled thud of a shovel or pick had reached them and alerted them to danger. Perhaps, too, the report from the forward observers was ill-founded. He would have to find out.

He worked his way to the advance rifle pits and questioned the soldiers there. What, exactly, had they seen? They had seen a detail of the enemy, with spades, apparently digging at several locations behind the earthworks of the fort. How many men? Perhaps twenty or more. It was hard to tell, for they were mostly hidden, but their actions were suspicious.

Peering cautiously above the trench, Pleasants glued his eyes steadily on the fort for several minutes. He could see nothing to confirm the report, but he was gloomily convinced that what he had been told was not a product of fancy. The matter needed further investigation, but meanwhile, he decided, the digging of the lateral galleries should proceed.

That night, around midnight, Pleasants ordered everyone out of the tunnel. Then he routed from sleep Captain William Winlack, the C Company commander, and ordered him and one of his men to accompany him. The three entered the mine, without lights, and cautiously made their way along the full length of the main gallery. At the far end, Pleasants motioned Captain Winlack to follow the right lateral gallery to its extremity, and the other man to follow the left. Lying face down, ears to the ground, each man then remained motionless, in absolute darkness and perfect silence, listening for any slightest sound that would give evidence of operations going on above.

Thirty minutes passed. Then, with a low whistle, Pleasants summoned his two companions from the lateral galleries, and the three stood together for a moment. Nothing had disturbed the profound stillness, not even the sound of musket fire that occasionally came at that hour from the fort.

Whispering into Winlack's ear, Pleasants said: "What do you think about any counterboring?"

"I don't think the Rebels know any more about this tunnel being under them than the inhabitants of Africa do," Winlack whispered back.

"That's just what I believe," breathed Pleasants. Then, turning to the other man, he said, "What's your opinion?"

75

The reply was softly spoken. Pleasants didn't catch it, and leaned closer. Again the reply was unintelligible. Then the tension that had been growing tighter and tighter within him suddenly snapped in a burst of fury.

"Good God, man!" he roared. "Why do you mumble your words? Speak out so I can understand you!"

The strident voice rang from one end of the gallery to the other, to be followed by a shocked silence. Instantly realizing what he had done, Pleasants was sick with the guilt of having rashly violated his own mandates of caution, and with the worry of having possibly ruined the whole operation on which so many men had labored so hard. Without another word he led the way out of the tunnel, pausing at the exit to grip the arms of Captain Winlack and his man in a gesture of apology and regret.

Contritely he went to his tent and lay down, wondering what would be the price of his folly. If, as Captain Winlack had said, the Rebels were completely ignorant of the mine operation, how much did they know *now?* What sentry, half dozing at his post in the fort, may have been startled by the subterranean outburst, and at this very moment might be communicating the discovery to an officer? Poor Burnside! What recriminations might descend on *him* if the whole operation fell through?

But next day, after his sleepless night, Pleasants ordered excavation to be resumed in the lateral galleries. Four days later, July 22, work on the left lateral was completed. Less than twenty-four hours later the right lateral was finished. Each of these galleries was provided with a powder chamber to contain the explosive.

At long last the job was done. It had taken 400 men four weeks of hard labor. Fewer men could have done it in much less time if they had been given adequate and proper equipment, but they had had to get along with such makeshift tools and implements as could be devised and scrounged in the difficult circumstances. No matter; they had accomplished what they had set out to do—what the top command in the Headquarters at City Point had said could not be done.

Pleasants was immensely proud of them, proud of this sinister achievement begotten of their toil. Meticulously, for the official record that he knew army protocol would demand, he checked and rechecked the dimensions of the tunnel, jotting down the figures on the back of an old envelope:

"Main gallery, 511.8 feet; right lateral, 38 feet; left lateral, 37 feet; total length of excavations 586.8 feet. Check.

Height of all galleries, varying from four to five feet and more; width, around five feet; volume of material excavated, about 18,000 cubic feet. Check."

The date was Saturday, July 23, 1864. The hour was 6:30 P.M. He went to his tent, wiped the perspiration from his face with a filthy towel, and stretched out on his cot. Tomorrow he would find out about the powder.

8

Improvise—or Else!

During the four weeks that the tunnel was being dug, other events destined to have some bearing on the mine operation were transpiring elsewhere. Every hour that passed following the 17th of June saw the Confederate defenses of Petersburg strengthened by wire, entrenchments, better trained troops, and increased fire power. In the same way, Union strategy directing the siege was busily applied to the question of whether a direct offensive should be launched in conjunction with the exploding of the mine— assuming that the tunnel operation *was* successful, and the mine *could* be exploded. If a direct offensive were decided upon, then there were other questions to be answered: When should the attack be made? Who was to lead it and what units were to be involved? Where, exactly, was the proper point at which to attack?

Since Burnside's Ninth Corps was in close proximity to the enemy, and the 48th Regiment of Potter's Second Division closest of any Federal unit, it would seem that this salient was the logical springboard for a direct assault. There was one disadvantage, however, in that any troops attacking from this advanced position would be conspicuously exposed to a murderous enfilade. Even if the explosion was successful, and Pegram's battery was knocked out, other batteries in the Confederate fortifications could command a sweeping field of fire against a frontal attack at this point. Another disadvantage was the uphill slope to the fort, and, beyond that, the sharp rise of ground that would have to be covered before the crest of Cemetery Hill was gained.

These were factors that had to be weighed carefully, and doubtless there were others. Apparently the consideration of them left no time for the more immediate problems which Colonel Pleasants was encountering. Strangely enough, Headquarters bespoke no faith whatever in the mine, and offered no assistance, yet behaved in a manner that seemed to indicate it expected nothing short of complete success. As early as July 3, scarcely more than a week after Meade was apprised of the mine operation in the message from Burnside, Grant was pondering plans for an offensive, and conferring with Meade on the subject. What, Grant suddenly wanted to know, were Burnside's views on the matter? Meade got in touch with Burnside, and in the exchange of correspondence there was established some enlightening documentary evidence of petty egoism in uniform.

"Headquarters Army of the Potomac
12 M. July 3, 1864

The lieutenant general commanding has inquired of me whether an assault on the enemy's works is practicable and feasible at any part of the line held by this army. In order to enable me to reply to this inquiry, I desire, at your earliest convenience, your views as to the practicability of an assault at any point in your front, to be made by the 2nd and 6th Corps in conjunction with yours.

Respectfully,
George G. Meade, Major General
Major General Burnside"

79

Burnside's reply to Meade was prompt and forthright:

"Headquarters, Ninth Army Corps
July 3, 1864

I have delayed answering your dispatch until I could get the opinion of my division commanders, and have another reconnaissance of the lines made by one of my staff. If my opinion is required as to whether now is the best time to make an assault, it being understood that if not made the siege is to continue, I should unhesitatingly say, wait until the mine is finished.

If the question is between making the assault now and a change of plan looking to operations in other quarters, I should unhesitatingly say, assault now. If the assault be delayed until the completion of the mine, I think we should have a more even chance of success. If the assault can be made now, I think we have a fair chance of success provided my corps can make the attack, and it is left to me to say when and how the other two corps shall come in to my support.

I have the honor to be, general, very respectfully your obedient servant

A. E. Burnside,
Major General Commanding 9th Corps
Major General Meade,
Commanding Army of the Potomac"

General Meade must have read this letter several times over. No doubt he found it well worded, comprehensive, and properly noncommittal. All that Burnside asked was that he be given control of the disposition of supporting troops in the event that the assault was made. Certainly this was not unreasonable. And yet the missive got deeply under Meade's skin.

In his testimony later before the Congressional Committee on the Conduct of the War, Burnside magnanimously stated that his wording of the letter was perhaps unfortunate, and that it was open to misconstruction. Meade's reply indicated that he had given it the worst possible interpretation:

"Headquarters Army of the Potomac
July 3, 1864

General: Your note by Major Lydig has been received. As you are of the opinion there is a reasonable degree of probability of success from an assault on your front, I shall so report to the lieutenant general commanding, and await his instructions.

The recent operations in your front, as you are aware, though sanctioned by me, did not originate in any orders from these headquarters. Should it, however, be determined to employ the army under my command in offensive operations on your front, I shall exercise the prerogative of my position to control and direct the same, receiving gladly at all times such suggestions as you may think proper to make. I consider these remarks necessary in consequence of certain conditions which you have thought proper to attach to your opinion, acceding to which in advance would not, in my judgment, be consistent with my position as commanding general of this army. I have accordingly directed Major Duane, chief engineer, and Brigadier General Hunt, chief of artillery, to make an examination of your lines, and to confer with you as to the operations to be carried on, the running of the mine now in progress, and the posting of artillery. It is advisable as many guns as possible, bearing on the point to be assaulted, should be in position.

I agree with you in opinion that the assault should be deferred till the mine is completed, provided that can be done within a reasonably short period,—say a week. Roads should be opened to the rear to facilitate the movements of the other corps sent to take part in the action, and all the preliminary arrangements possible should be made. Upon the reports of my engineer and artillery officers, the necessary orders will be given.

Respectfully yours,

Geo. G. Meade, Major General Commanding
Major General Burnside
Commanding 9th Corps"

Just as Meade had insisted on interpreting Burnside's letter as a personal affront, Burnside now viewed Meade's answer as an uncalled-for reproof. Both officers were equally sensitive, although Meade's superior rank gave him greater license to sensitivity. It was therefore incumbent upon Burnside to assume a posture of apology, and this he did with all the gentlemanly control of which he was capable, while doubtless seething with anger inwardly.

"Headquarters 9th Army Corps
July 4, 1864

General: I have the honor to acknowledge the receipt of your letter of last evening, and am very sorry that I should have been so unfortunate in expressing myself in my letter. It was written in haste, after just receiving the necessary data upon which to strengthen an opinion already pretty well formed. I assure you, in all candor, that I never dreamed of implying any lack of confidence in your ability to do all that is necessary in any grand movement which may be undertaken by your army. Were you to personally direct an attack from my front, I would feel the utmost confidence; and were I called upon to support an attack from the front of the 2nd and 6th Corps, directed by yourself, or by either of the commanders of those corps, I would do it with confidence and cheerfulness.

It is hardly necessary for me to say that I have had

the utmost faith in your ability to handle troops ever since my acquaintance with you in the Army of the Potomac, and certainly accord you a much higher position in the art of war than I possess; and I, at the same time, entertain the greatest respect for the skill of the two gentlemen commanding the 2nd and 6th Corps; so that my duty to my country, and to you, and to myself, forbids that I should for a moment assume to embarrass you, or them, by an assumption of position or authority. I simply desired to ask the privilege of calling upon them for support at such times, and at such points, as I thought advisable. I would gladly accord to either of them the same support, and would be glad to have either of them lead the attack; but it would have been obviously improper for me to have suggested that any other corps than my own should make the attack in my front. What I asked, in reference to calling upon the other corps for support, is only what I have been called upon to do, and have cheerfully done myself, in regard to other corps commanders.

If a copy of my letter has been forwarded to the General-in-Chief, which I take for granted has been done, that he may possess my full opinion, it may make the same impression upon him as upon yourself; and I beg that you will correct it; in fact, I beg that such impression may be, as far as possible, removed wherever it has made a lodgment. My desire is to support you, and in doing that I am serving my country.

With ordinary good fortune, we can safely promise to finish the mine in a week; I hope in less time.

I have the honor to be, general, very respectfully, your obedient servant,

A. E. Burnside,

Major General Commanding 9th Army Corps

Major General Meade
Commanding Army of the Potomac"

From the foregoing, it appears that General Burnside was extremely anxious to placate Meade, and that he was really asking only for the authority to meet such emergencies as might arise suddenly and require immediate decision. He knew from experience that time consumed in going through military channels could, in some situations, jeopardize lives and defeat aims. He also knew that Meade was a stickler for protocol, that he was inflexible in his insistence on regulations. Perhaps what he did not know before, but had now found out, was the size of the chip perched precariously on the two-star epaulette of the Commanding General of the Army of the Potomac. Burnside's expressed concern for the impression his letter may have made upon Grant appears to be genuine. Actually, it may have been a gesture made in mockery. In any case, Meade accepted it at face value, and sent reassurances:

"Headquarters Army of the Potomac
July 4, 1864

General: Your letter of this date is received. I am glad to find that there was no intention on your part to ask for any more authority and command than you have a perfect right to expect under existing circumstances. I did not infer from your letter that you had any want of confidence in me. I rather thought you were anticipating interference from others, and thought it best to reply as I did.

Your letter has not been shown to anyone, nor forwarded to the General-in-Chief, and my answer has only been seen by the confidential clerk who copied it. I am very grateful to you for your good opinion, as expressed, and shall earnestly try to merit its continuance. In the trying position I am placed in, hardly to be appreciated by anyone not in my place, it is my great desire to be on terms of harmony and good feel-

84

ing with all, superiors and subordinates; and I try to adjust the little jars that will always exist in large bodies to the satisfaction of each one. I have no doubt, by frankness and full explanations, such as have now taken place between us, all misapprehensions will be removed. You may rest assured, all the respect due to your rank and position will be paid you while under my command.

Truly yours,

George G. Meade, Major General"

Actually, General Meade was not being anywhere near as magnanimous as this letter makes him appear. It would have been far better for Burnside, and for the whole Union cause, if the Ninth Corps Commander's letter of July 3 and Meade's reply of the same date had been forwarded to Grant, as they certainly should have been. It may be that Burnside had counted on this, had conducted his end of the exchange of correspondence in such a way as to flag Grant's attention to Meade's aloof and uncooperative attitude. Possibly Burnside felt that if Grant personally interested himself in this matter, and took steps to correct Meade's unreasonable position in regard to the assault plans, he might also discover that Meade was not cooperating in the mine operation, and do something about that.

As it was, Grant may have heard of Meade's lack of cooperation for the first time when, months later, Colonel Pleasants was obliged to testify before the Congressional Committee on the Conduct of the War. In that official inquiry, Pleasants would be asked why he had not been able to procure better instruments with which to construct his tunnel. His reply would be honest and forthright:

"I do not know. Whenever I made application I could not get anything, although General Burnside was very favorable to it. The most important thing was to ascertain

85

how far I had to mine, because if I fell short of or went beyond the proper place the explosion would have no practical effect. Therefore, I wanted an accurate instrument with which to make the necessary triangulations. I had to make them on the furthest front line, where the enemy sharpshooters could reach me. I could not get the instrument I wanted, although there was one at army headquarters; and General Burnside had to send to Washington and get an old-fashioned theodolite, which was given to me."

Did Colonel Pleasants know any reason why he could not have had the better theodolite which was at Headquarters? Again the bold reply that must have made Meade wince and Grant raise his eyebrows:

"I do not. I know this: that General Burnside told me that General Meade and Major Duane, Chief Engineer of the Army of the Potomac, said the thing could not be done; that it was all claptrap and nonsense; that such a length of mine had never been excavated in military operations, and could not be; that I should either get the men smothered for want of air or crushed by the falling of the earth, or the enemy would find it out, and it would amount to nothing. I could get no boards and lumber supplied to me for my operations. I had to get a pass, and send two companies of my own regiment with wagons outside of our lines to Rebel sawmills and get lumber in that way, after having previously got what lumber I could by tearing down an old bridge. I had no mining picks furnished me, but had to take common picks and have them straightened for my mining picks."

Would Colonel Pleasants say that General Burnside was the only officer who seemed to favor the mine? Pleasants would and did:

"The only officer of high rank, so far as I learned. General Burnside, corps commander, and General Potter, the division commander, seemed to be the only high officers who believed in it."

Could Colonel Pleasants estimate how much time might have been saved in constructing the mine if he had been supplied with the proper tools and instruments? Indeed Pleasants was to say, in truth and bitterness:

"I could have done it in one third or one fourth of the time. The greatest cause of the delay was taking the material out. We had to carry it the whole length of the mine, to where it could be deposited, and every night I had to get the pioneers of my regiment to cut bushes and cover it up where it had been deposited. Otherwise the enemy could have climbed up the trees in their lines and seen the newly excavated earth."

. . . But all this was in the future. In that month of July, 1864, the protests of a mere brigade leader could not be heard in the higher echelons. The words of a brigadier general could be twisted by a major general, or simply suppressed. There could be kinks in a chain of command, obstructions in channels of communication. And the highest ranking leader in uniform could be ignorant of things he ought to know.

In the Headquarters at City Point, General Ulysses S. Grant was busy poring over reports, making plans, issuing orders. After five weeks of comparatively little action, he was heartily stimulated by the prospect of a major offensive. It would be touched off by Burnside's mine (everybody was calling it Burnside's mine, these days) and followed by a smashing blow that ought to put Petersburg in his pocket very shortly. It promises to be, he confided to Meade, the most successful assault of the campaign.

9

"Please Sign Here, Sir"

Sunday morning, July 24, Colonel Pleasants got word through to General Burnside that the mine was ready to be charged, and suggested that Headquarters be notified and arrangements made to furnish the necessary supply of powder. Burnside wanted to know how much powder, and Pleasants reckoned they would need about twelve thousand pounds. Other materials would be required, too, he pointed out—wire and fuses, sandbags for tamping, and a galvanic battery. He had jotted everything down neatly in a list, as a housewife going to the corner grocery might do, and Burnside said he would give it his immediate attention.

When the requisition was forwarded to Headquarters, however, there was loud dissension from Major Duane and his staff. A much smaller quantity of powder would be sufficient, they said, to do the job. In fact, too heavy a charge would tend to localize severely the effects of the blast; more widespread damage would result if a lighter charge were used. While the argument went on at Headquarters, vigorously debated by officers who had never taken the trouble to inspect the mine tunnel, Burnside's attention was diverted to another matter.

From Major General A. A. Humphreys, Meade's chief of staff, came a note requesting a detailed statement of the plan of attack from Burnside's front. Also, Humphreys said,

Meade wanted to know whether anything had transpired to give substance to the rumor of countermining by the enemy. If so, Meade wanted the mine charged and sprung as quickly as possible. Otherwise the blast should be deferred until it could be coupled with "other operations."

In regard to the countermining, Burnside had to admit that it was now more fact than rumor. A number of deserters from the enemy had been picked up, and from them it was learned that the Rebels inside the big redoubt on the hill were indeed sinking shafts in an effort to locate the mine. The deserters said that no one had any positive knowledge of the existence of a mine, but that there was considerable suspicion on that subject, and Confederate engineers were trying hard to prove or disprove that suspicion.

Burnside informed Meade fully of these developments, but gave the impression that it was not likely the enemy would succeed in sending an intersecting shaft into the tunnel just yet. More imminently dangerous, he said, was the possibility of a cave-in in the left lateral gallery of the tunnel. It was directly over this lateral that Pegram's batteries were stationed, and it had been discovered that every time the big guns were fired, the roof of this gallery trembled ominously from the shock. Pleasants had rushed shoring timbers to this weak spot, and the roof had been heavily bolstered. Nevertheless, Burnside told Meade, "it is highly important, in my opinion, that the mine should be exploded at the earliest possible moment consistent with the general interests of the campaign." He added that Meade himself must choose the day for the explosion, but that his own feeling was that the charge should be set off just before daylight, or around five o'clock in the afternoon, of the day selected.

As to his plan of attack, Burnside was well prepared to give Meade the detailed statement he requested. He had been at work on those details for some time, had rehearsed them carefully in his mind until he could envision the precise movements of the troops assigned to the assault. Now his pen flowed smoothly over the paper as he communicated the arrangements to Meade.

"My plan," he wrote, "would be to . . . mass the two brigades of the colored division in rear of my first line in columns of division 'double columns closed in mass,' the head of each brigade resting on the front line, and, as soon as the explosion has taken place, move them forward with instructions for the division to take half distance, and as soon as the leading regiments of the two brigades pass through the gap in the enemy's line, the leading regiments of the right brigade to come into line perpendicular to the enemy's line by the 'right companies on the right into line, wheel,' the 'left companies on the right into line,' and proceed at once down the line of the enemy's works as rapidly as possible; and the leading regiment of the left brigade to execute the reverse movement to the left, moving up the enemy's line. The remainder of the columns to move directly toward the crest in front as rapidly as possible, diverging in such a way as to enable them to deploy in columns of regiment, the right column making as nearly as possible for Cemetery Hill. These columns to be followed by the other divisions of the other corps as soon as they can be thrown in.

"This would involve the necessity of relieving these divisions by other troops before the movement, and of holding columns of other troops in readiness to take our place on the crest in case we gain it, and sweep down it. It would, in my opinion, be advisable, if we succeed in gaining the crest, to throw the colored division right into the town. There is a necessity for the co-operation, at least in the way of artillery, by the troops on our right and left. Of the extent of this you will necessarily be the judge. I think our chances of success in a plan of this kind are more than even. . . ."

The colored division Burnside referred to was one of the four divisions comprising the Ninth Corps, and was made up entirely of Negro troops—more than 4,000 strong—under the command of Brigadier General Edward Ferrero. In contrast to the 1st, 2nd, and 3rd Divisions of the Ninth Corps, this 4th Division was uniquely fresh. It had been recruited in Philadelphia less than a year previously, and its personnel, under white officers, had been engaged mostly in rear-guard duty. Some few units had been tried in combat during the storming of the enemy's advanced works, and had acquitted themselves well. Ferrero had not distinguished himself in any phase of campaigning up to this time, but he was considered extremely capable, and well liked by his subordinate officers and men. Early in July, Burnside had officially notified Ferrero that his 4th Division was being assigned to carry the assault of Petersburg in the wake of the mine blast, although at that time Burnside could not be sure that this would meet with Meade's approval. The Corps Commander had merely wanted to be prepared for the day when Headquarters would abruptly demand of him what provisions he had made to follow up the explosion—and now the question had been asked, and his answer was ready.

That answer, phrased in the peculiar military jargon of the era, may require translation in order to be understood by the laity of today. Briefly, what Burnside was saying was that the 4th Division was to be poised for action when the mine was fired, and that as soon as the explosion had breached the enemy's line these Negro troops were to move forward, up the slope toward the fort—or what would be left of it—and attack to the right and left so as to widen the breach already made. The other divisions of Burnside's corps were to follow, fanning out to smother any remaining opposition, after which all remaining forces were to push forward and onward to the coveted strong point of Cemetery Hill. The plan seemed virtually foolproof to Burnside, and only restraining modesty dictated the limit of his optimism in the statement: "I think our chances of success in a plan of this kind are more than even." What Meade and Grant would think of the chances remained to be seen.

At the moment, Grant's head was buzzing with other ideas. He was essentially a man of action, and he had not been enjoying the enforced idleness of the siege any more than the lowliest soldier of his command. For some days, ever since Meade had diffidently informed him that Burnside's mine appeared to be progressing satisfactorily, he had been pleasantly engaged in plotting the course of the offensive that seemed to be so happily opportune. Perhaps things were going to work out right, after all. Perhaps the bigwigs in Washington, who had plainly been puzzled by his failure to capture Petersburg, would have their eyes opened when the static front flamed with action; and the Northern press, which had begun to be openly critical, would have to do an about-face. Grant, they might say, has shown the gristle we knew he had all along. Grant knows what he is doing.

So, on Monday, July 25, while Meade and Duane were trying to decide how much powder to send to Burnside, Grant ordered Hancock's Second Corps infantry and three divisions of Sheridan's cavalry to make a diversionary expedition back across the James River. Ostensibly, the purpose of this maneuver was to raid railway lines between Petersburg and Richmond, and perhaps make a jab at Richmond itself if conditions warranted it. But actually Grant was again indulging in feinting tactics—the kind of movement he had created when he sent Warren forward across the Chickahominy to engage the enemy while the rest of the Army of the Potomac was withdrawing from the Wilderness. It was the kind of strategy that afforded him great satisfaction.

This time Hancock and Sheridan were the decoys. They were to move their troops with as much secrecy as possible —not to avoid detection, but to give the appearance of trying to do so. Observing the movement, General Lee would undoubtedly detach some of his forces from the Petersburg lines and seek to pursue and cut off, or drive back, this unexpected thrust at the Confederate capital. Thus, Grant mused, the Petersburg defenses would be materially weakened and the time would be ripe to explode "Burnside's mine" and strike the lethal blow at the beleaguered city.

The ruse worked just as Grant anticipated. Hancock's Second Corps crossed the James on a pontoon bridge at Deep Bottom, the extremity of the Union lines, early on the morning of Wednesday, the 27th. By that time, Lee had sent three divisions of infantry to meet this new threat, and followed up swiftly with still another infantry division and two divisions of cavalry, all withdrawn from Petersburg's defense. Following orders, Hancock made no effort to attack such a vastly superior force, and on the night of Friday, the 29th, he simply fell back, withdrew his entire corps to the south side of the James, and waited for further developments.

Grant had observed all of this cumbersome byplay with patience and deep interest. Now he applied himself to a simple arithmetical problem. From the number of known enemy divisions that had been mustered to the defense of Petersburg he subtracted those divisions which Lee had pulled out to intercept Hancock. The result showed that Petersburg must now contain no more than three divisions of infantry and one of cavalry. This knowledge, coupled with some observations Hancock had made on the north side of the James regarding a lack of continuity in some of

93

the Rebel lines of entrenchment, convinced Grant that the iron was hot, and that the time had come to strike. He checked with Meade: had the powder been sent to Burnside? Was the mine ready to be sprung? If so, he wanted it sprung next day, as early as possible—say, 3:30 in the morning.

The powder had indeed been delivered, but not before Colonel Henry Pleasants had been subjected to the most agonizing delay he had yet encountered in this campaign. Some time before the mine was completed on July 23, Burnside had ascertained that the powder would be available quickly, from Fortress Monroe, when the exact quantity desired was made known. When, on the 24th, the requisition for 12,000 pounds became the subject of dispute at Headquarters, Pleasants knew nothing about what was causing the delay. For the next three days he was in a torment of anxiety, scurrying back and forth between the tunnel, where he was supervising construction of powder magazines and their connecting tubes, and Burnside's tent, where he momentarily expected to hear that the powder was on its way.

Much of his anxiety was due to the now well-authenticated reports of enemy counterboring. Some of his men working in the lateral galleries had heard unmistakable sounds of digging overhead. If one thrust of a digging iron should penetrate the roof of the tunnel, all of the stupendous efforts of the 48th Regiment would be fruitless. Again and again he appealed to Burnside. What was delaying the powder? The Corps Commander, his own face haggard and drawn with anxiety, said that Headquarters was busy with plans for the offensive, and was apparently not yet ready to spring the mine.

"I can't understand it, Colonel Pleasants," he added. "I have literally prayed to Meade to get us the powder. The only thing that has saved us so far, I believe, is that the

Confederates have an idea that our mining operations are farther to the southwest, near the Jerusalem Plank Road. There they are doing a lot of countermining. If we could only get some action!"

Still the powder did not arrive, and all that Pleasants could do was make sure that everything was in readiness to handle it when Meade did see fit to deliver. He checked the system over and over. It consisted of eight magazines, constructed in the form of big wooden boxes, evenly spaced along both lateral galleries. The magazines were connected by wooden troughs, which converged at the point where the laterals joined the main gallery. The powder would be dumped into the magazines, and the troughs would be partly filled with powder. Where the troughs converged, wires were to be connected and run out through the mine to a galvanic battery. Then sandbags would be used to seal the tunnel at a point near the lateral galleries, thus tamping the charge, and a spark from the battery would do the rest. Fuses would be laid, too, so that if the battery failed to function, the charge could still be set off. Everything was in readiness, and now there was little to do but endure the ordeal of waiting as calmly as possible.

More as an exercise in self-control than anything else, Pleasants completed the writing of a letter to his uncle back in Rockland. He had started the letter on Sunday, the 23rd, laid it aside to supervise work in the final hours of excavation, and now finished it.

> "I have worked harder of late with body and brain than I ever did in my life before, [he wrote]. I have projected, undertaken and completed a gigantic work; and have accomplished one of the greatest things in this war. I have excavated a mine gallery from our line to and under the enemy's works. This mine is 511 feet in length, and has lateral galleries of 75 feet, making a total distance of 586 feet.

I am under one of their principal forts, and as soon as the 'high authorities' are ready, will put 12,000 (twelve thousand) lbs. of powder in 9 [sic] enormous magazines and will blow fort, cannon and rebels to the clouds.

The chief engineer of the Army and the rest of the regular army wiseacres said it was not feasible; that I could not carry the ventilation that distance without digging a hole to the surface, and that I would either get the men crushed by fall of earth, or have them smothered.

Old Burnside stood by me. Told me to go ahead and I have succeeded.

When I began I had neither an inch of board or a single nail. I caused our big picks to be made smaller; got cracker boxes, and made hand barrows out of them, and went ahead day and night until I finished it.

I now wait the order to put in the powder and reap the fruits of the work. It is terrible, however, to hurl several men with my own hand at one blow into eternity, but I believe I am doing right.

Be sure not to speak of this matter outside of Uncle James and Aunt Emily, until the thing is done:—then I will give you a fuller account."

He felt better when this missive had been dispatched. He had toiled so long against disheartening odds, had struggled so hard against stupid, thick-headed opposition, that it was a relief to communicate with someone who he knew would be filled with sympathetic understanding of what he had gone through, and admiration for what he had achieved. He knew, better than anyone else, that he had done a good job. Perhaps it was juvenile to boast about it, but there was a therapeutic value in the boasting. Somehow it helped to offset the gnawing bitterness of frustration over the interminable delays.

Early on Thursday, the 28th, came a brief note routed to Pleasants through Burnside. The powder had arrived at last! Pleasants rushed to a wooded covert well back in the Union lines, which had been designated as a rendezvous for the ammunition train of mule-drawn wagons. Sure enough, there it was, in ominous black kegs. He counted them twice —320 kegs, 25 pounds to the keg. But that came to only 8,000 pounds!

"Where is the rest?" he demanded of the lieutenant in charge of the train. "We requisitioned twelve thousand pounds. Where's the rest of it?"

"I don't know, sir," the lieutenant said, squirming uncomfortably under the fierce gleam in his superior's eye. "My orders call for just this consignment."

"But I requisitioned twelve thousand pounds, lieutenant. You're exactly one hundred sixty kegs short."

"I'm sorry, sir. If there's a mistake, I'm sure Headquarters will correct it. But this invoice calls for only eight thousand pounds. Will you please sign here, sir?"

He scribbled his signature in a hand that shook with anger. Then he told Sergeant Reese to assemble a detail and have the kegs carried into the mine. He himself stormed off to Corps headquarters.

"I'm afraid," Burnside said soothingly, "that nothing can be done about it, Colonel. The requisition for twelve thousand pounds was definitely disapproved by Meade. I've known all along that they were going to reduce it, but I had hoped they would give us more than this. Do you think it may suffice?"

Suffice? Well, if nothing could be done about it, it would damn well have to suffice! Back he went to the tunnel to supervise the unloading of the kegs and the distribution of the powder.

It was slow work, carrying the kegs the full length of the main gallery, opening them, dumping the powder into the magazines and spilling it along the connecting troughs. Dangerous work, too, that had to be done in the dark; no lanterns or torches allowed! Before it had progressed very far Pleasants called an abrupt halt. Some of the men carrying the powder to the magazines had felt their boots cake with mud. They mentioned it to Sergeant Reese, who promptly reported to Pleasants. Investigation showed that a dismaying amount of water seepage had been taking place in the two lateral galleries. The wooden magazines were resting squarely on the sodden floor, and their sides were already damp, through and through, as much as a foot above the ground.

Grimly Pleasants tackled the job of raising the magazines on wooden supports, and elevating the connecting troughs several inches from the floor. At all costs, the powder had to be kept dry. By the time these precautions had been taken and the dumping of the powder resumed, evening had come on.

No date had yet been officially announced for exploding the mine, but Burnside had indicated that word might come very suddenly and that he wanted everything ready for firing as quickly as possible. Grant, he said, was deploying some infantry and cavalry divisions on the other side of the James, and he had a hunch that this might be the prelude to the order for springing the mine and launching the all-out offensive. Burnside was palpably nervous; so much depended on him. And Pleasants was jittery, too, because Burnside had placed responsibility for the whole mine operation on his shoulders.

Now came word that the galvanic battery and wire had not arrived, but that delivery had just been made of the sandbags and fuses. Pleasants was in the mine when the message came. He hurried outside to find Captain Hoskings, now commanding the 48th, standing in a clump of trees with some other officers. They were all looking down at a burlap-covered bale, one end of which had been ripped open to expose a section of fuse.

"At last!" Pleasants burst out in relief. "They really did get us the fuse, didn't they?"

"Yes, but look at it, Colonel." Captain Hoskings reached down and drew up a coil, shaking his head glumly. "This is just common blasting fuse, and it's all cut up into short lengths, some of them only ten feet long."

Pleasants stared dumbly at the thin coil of fuse in Hoskings' extended hand. Then he turned away for a moment, folded his arms quietly across his chest, and leaned wearily against the bullet-scarred trunk of the nearest tree, facing in the direction of City Point, three miles away. There was a long and awkward silence, broken only by the thud of the coiled fuse as Hoskings tossed it on the ground. Then, without turning around, Pleasants said in a voice choked with emotion:

"I asked for three sections, each five hundred feet long. Why can't the stupid blockheads do something *right*—just once?"

"It'll be a lot of work to splice it," Hoskings muttered, "but I suppose it can be done. . . ."

"We've got to start on it, right now," Pleasants said in a calmer voice. "But this time I'm going back at them."

On his own authority he sent two men immediately to City Point, with instructions to convey to Major Duane or one of Meade's own aides his sharply worded note of dissatisfaction and the request that his original requisition for fuse be filled at once, if possible. Then he had Hoskings summon the practical miners of the 48th and set them to work splicing the short lengths. It was something they knew how to do, but it needed to be done carefully, and it was time consuming. That evening the job was done, just as the two messengers returned from the laborious trip to City Point to report that Headquarters of the Army of the Potomac had been unable to procure the desired type of fuse and was plainly annoyed at the forthright demand for it.

Annoyed? Well, let them be! He and every officer and man in the 48th had sweated blood to get this job done, and mere annoyance was of no account.

The first lengths of spliced fuse had been connected, as soon as ready, with the troughs leading to the powder magazines, and then, while additional pieces were spliced to stretch out through the main gallery to the tunnel exit, tamping was begun. From the point where it opened out into the laterals, the main gallery was filled for a distance of forty feet with tightly packed sandbags and earth, interspersed with logs in a way that would admit sufficient oxygen to augment the explosion. Tamping and fuse splicing were finished at about the same time, on the evening of Thursday, the 28th. And with that, the whole business was completed. Incredibly, the last tap of work had been done, the loaded galleries sealed, and everything was ready.

Before reporting to General Burnside, Pleasants made a final round of inspection with Sergeant Reese and Lieutenant Douty. They checked the triple line of fuse, snugly wrapped in waterproofed material, all the way from the exit of the tunnel to where it disappeared into the tamping. Beyond that point, nothing could be done. Everything on the other side of the tamping had already been checked. Walking back through the tunnel, they ran their hands over the fuse again, followed it to the exit, and outside, where an upturned box had been placed over the terminals. Two soldiers guarding the box saluted.

The five men stood there for a minute in the darkness, looking out over the terrain toward the enemy fort on the slope, with the silhouette of Cemetery Hill beyond. Under that fort lay a slumbering giant of destruction, waiting to be aroused.

"All we need now is a match," Colonel Pleasants breathed softly.

But the time to apply the match had not yet been set, and Pleasants went to bed that night with a terrible burden of uneasiness. The mine was ready and waiting to be sprung, but if there were to be any substantial delay in springing it, something would surely go wrong. He tossed restlessly on his cot, too exhausted and worried after the day's trials to find the sleep he sorely needed.

Not far away, at Corps Headquarters, General Burnside was spending an equally sleepless night. It had been a trying day for him, too. The details of charging the mine—the whole complicated business of the powder, the fuses, the tamping—he had left in the hands of Colonel Pleasants. His own personal concern was properly focused on the attack which was to be launched from his front, and although his plans for this attack were fully complete and crystal clear, he had this day received disquieting news with respect to them. And for the first time since that evening more than a month ago, when General Potter and his young brigade commander had called on him to discuss the proposed mine operation, the Ninth Corps commander had a premonition of disaster.

10

Three Blades of Grass

What had occurred to disturb General Burnside so pro-
foundly originated Thursday morning, July 28, with a note
from General Meade, asking him to come to his headquarters immediately. The message was not unexpected. Evi-
dently the moment had arrived when Meade wished to an-
nounce the date for exploding the mine.

In a high spirit of anticipation, Burnside called on the
commanding major general. Meade was waiting for him,
and discussed at some length the maneuver by Hancock's
Second Corps across the river. He said Hancock had skir-
mished with the enemy and inflicted some damage, but
would not continue to advance beyond his present position;
that Grant would in all probability order Hancock to withdraw within another twenty-four hours. The important
thing about all this, Meade said, was that Lee had sent so
many troops out of Petersburg's fortifications to intercept
Hancock that the city's defenses were pretty weak right
now. Then he asked:

"How long will it take to charge that mine?"

"It's being charged right now," Burnside said. "I should
think Colonel Pleasants would have the job finished by to-
night."

"Very good. Now, about your plan of attack. I cannot
approve of your placing the Negro troops in the advance,
as proposed in your project."

Burnside sat up very straight in his camp chair. "May I ask why, sir?"

"Because I think the task is much too important to be entrusted to them. At any rate, they should certainly not lead the attack."

"But General," Burnside spread his hands in a gesture of helplessness, "my three other divisions have been in the front lines, under fire almost ceaselessly for the past six weeks. They have suffered a good many casualties. They're not in the best of condition, unfortunately. Also, the constant harassment by sharpshooters, and the frequent bombardment from the enemy forts, has had its effect. They have had to stay under cover so much that a lot of their normal aggressiveness is lacking. On the other hand, the 4th Division colored troops . . ."

The discussion went on for some minutes. Over and over again, Burnside made the point that his 1st, 2nd, and 3rd Divisions had borne the brunt of the campaign so far, and were suffering combat fatigue—although that term had not yet been coined. He cited actual figures, totals of killed, wounded, and missing, to support his contention that these troops had suffered disproportionately, while the 4th Division was intact, fresh, and—above all—expressly alerted and prepared for the leading role in the assault.

Meade's strong face was impassive. He listened tolerantly but gave no evidence of changing his opinion. Finally he dismissed Burnside with assurances that he would take the matter up with General Grant during the afternoon and communicate Grant's decision that evening.

So, while Colonel Pleasants was tossing and turning on his bunk, plagued by nightmare worries over whether the mine might explode prematurely, or fill up with water and never explode at all, or cave in unexpectedly, or be discovered by Confederate engineers, Burnside was fretting over the threatened upset of his plan regarding the Negro

103

troops, and wondering how he could revise the plan if Grant wanted it revised. He had a lot to think about.

Almost from the moment the first bayonet was stabbed into the baked earth on the hillside below the Confederate fort, signaling the start of the mining operation, the question of which division of the Ninth Corps would have the honor of leading the attack following the explosion had been raised in every unit. Not unreasonably, the 48th Pennsylvania Regiment claimed priority in the matter. These men had a tenacious faith in their brigade leader who had originated and was promoting the mine operation, and regarded everything connected with this project as their unit responsibility.

As the project advanced, selection of the attacking division became imperative. Only by a carefully planned and properly rehearsed series of troop movements, following immediately after the explosion, would it be possible to take full advantage of the blast's paralyzing effect on the enemy, and the attendant collapse of discipline. Burnside therefore began reviewing the situation quite carefully long before he was directed to produce a plan of attack, but wisely in anticipation of that directive.

The Ninth Corps commander knew a thing or two about powder explosions. He visualized that when the mine was sprung there would be a dense cloud of smoke and dust hovering over the Confederate earthworks for at least half an hour. Through this cloud, the attacking division would be able to charge up the slope, across the depression caused by the blast, and on to Cemetery Hill, well screened from whatever direct or enfilade fire the enemy might be capable of turning loose. Actually, it was quite possible that the shock of the explosion would eliminate all fire power, and that the key point of the Petersburg defenses might fall into Union hands without a shot! Considering it in this light, Burnside felt that the leading assault force need not necessarily be comprised of seasoned veterans. Much more important than combat experience were fresh vigor, stamina, and enthusiasm.

He already had his mind set on the 4th Division colored troops when Colonel Pleasants respectfully requested that his own brigade, including the 48th Regiment, be allowed to spearhead the attack. Burnside rejected the request in no uncertain terms. Pleasants and his miners, he said, were laboring hard on the excavation of the tunnel. They would have neither the time to devote to preparations for the assault mission, nor the energy to carry out that mission after their work on the mine was completed. Besides, he added, it would be unfair to place so much duty and responsibility on one small segment of the Army when there were troops available that had been called upon for relatively little action thus far in the campaign.

So it was early in July that Burnside summoned Brigadier General Edward Ferrero and explained the part he had in mind for the 4th Division. Ferrero concurred readily, and, after receiving preliminary instructions, immediately set to work training his Negro troops for the assignment. News of this assignment was received with enthusiasm by the officers of the 4th Division. Most enthusiastic of all, perhaps, was Colonel Joshua K. Sigfried, former commanding officer of the 48th Regiment, who now commanded the 4th Division's First Brigade. He and Pleasants were fellow Schuylkill Countians and comrades in arms, and Sigfried had a keen personal interest in the mine project. He was an exceptionally fine leader, and now applied himself rigorously to the conditioning of his brigade for action.

The regiments in Sigfried's brigade were the 27th, Lieutenant Colonel Charles J. Wright commanding; 30th, Colonel Delevan Bates; 39th, Colonel Ozora P. Stearns; and 43rd, Lieutenant Colonel H. Seymour Hall.

The division's Second Brigade, commanded by Colonel

Henry Goddard Thomas, was made up of the 19th, Lieutenant Colonel Joseph G. Perkins; 23rd, Colonel Cleaveland J. Campbell; 28th, Lieutenant Colonel Charles S. Russell; 29th, Lieutenant Colonel John A. Brass; and 31st, Lieutenant Colonel W. E. W. Ross.

Numerically, the division was oversize, with a roster of 4,300—2,000 in Sigfried's Brigade, 2,300 in Thomas's.

While the officers were enthusiastic and elated over the division's assigned role in the assault, the effect on the men was markedly different. They were proud but sobered by the honor thrust upon them. Through oversimplified orientation they knew what the war was all about. They understood the present situation, and the impending developments. Months before they were put into uniform they had been told that Lincoln had abolished slavery with his Emancipation Proclamation. It was a little hard to understand how this could have been accomplished by a man writing words on a piece of paper; much easier to comprehend that this freedom might come through physical ordeal. Now they had been chosen to perform a spectacular act—one that in all probability would end the war and give the black man release from injustice and servitude forever—and there was something almost apocalyptic in this, something mysterious and deeply spiritual.

As the training of these troops got under way, their fervor took on a fanatical intensity. Each day one regiment was withdrawn to a point back of the lines and put through a drill in the tactics to be used in the assault. They participated in these rehearsals as though sharing in some great religious ceremony, their faces serious, almost reverent. In low, gruff voices, their burly noncommissioned officers relayed commands that brought precise response.

On several occasions Colonel Pleasants visited Colonel Sigfried and watched some of these regiments go through their routines.

"These boys are trained to the minute, Pleasants," Sigfried said one evening, a few days after the mine excavation was completed. "If that mine were to be exploded tomorrow morning, every soldier of my brigade would be in his place and do just what was expected of him. The whole command is on edge. The way they throw themselves into the drills, you'd think they were taking part in some strange, fantastic orgy. And look at them now!"

Campfires had been kindled in the company streets, and the Negroes sat around them in groups, their ebony faces shining in the flickering yellow light. One gigantic fellow, naked to the waist, stood up among them and began speaking in a low monotone, rich, musical, hypnotic. At intervals his great body quivered and bent forward in a crouch, arms and legs moving rhythmically. Then he stood erect, and broke into a deep bass chant:

> *We looks like men a-marchin' on,*
> *We looks like men o' war . . .*

As the melodious voice touched a low note, Pleasants was reminded of a magnificent violoncello in the hands of a musician he had once heard at a concert in Philadelphia. There was the same sonority and resonance, the same depth and vibration of tone, and they came now from a torso dark and gleaming as polished wood.

"Those men are entranced," Sigfried said softly. "They're doing what they call 'studying.' It's a sight to see, isn't it?"

But then the voice of the singer stirred them. One group joined in the chant, then another. In a few moments hundreds of men, up and down the company streets, in the tents, were uniting in a mighty chorus:

> *We looks like men a-marchin' on,*
> *We looks like men o' war . . .*

Pleasants felt the skin tingle along his arms and shoulders, and Sigfried muttered: "You see what I mean. I wouldn't want to be one of the enemy in the path of these fellows when they go up that slope!—even if they were armed only with clubs! And we've given them the best weapons we can get."

Burnside had been in close touch with Ferrero, and knew exactly how the Negroes were reacting, and how their training was coming along. He was confident that he had made a wise decision in committing the colored troops to the assault, and had had no hesitancy in communicating this decision to Headquarters in his written plan of attack, July 26. Now, on the night of the 28th, he was depressed by the interview he had had with Meade, and uneasy over the possibility that a message might arrive at any moment, telling him that Grant, too, had disapproved using the 4th Division.

But Friday the 29th dawned with no word received from Meade, and Burnside became optimistic. Around nine o'clock he sent for his 2nd and 3rd Division commanders, Generals Potter and Orlando B. Willcox, and the three discussed some of the details of their preparedness for the attack, whenever it was to take place. They agreed that a firm date would certainly be fixed soon, now that Hancock's sortie over the James had been halted. Speaking of what was heaviest on his mind, Burnside admitted that he had been greatly disturbed the day before by Meade's objection to the proposed use of the 4th Division, but that since no word to the contrary had reached him he was going to assume that everything was satisfactory as originally planned.

Potter and Willcox agreed that the 4th Division was the logical one to lead the assault, and reassured Burnside that Grant must undoubtedly be of the same mind. When Burnside dismissed them, they went over to the 48th Regiment's area to look at the mine and talked for a while with Pleasants.

"I take it everything is in good shape, Colonel," Potter said.

"As good as I know how to make it, sir," Pleasants replied earnestly. "I'm ready to blow it up as soon as I get the word."

"We'll probably get that word today," Potter said.

"I hope so, sir. What worries me is the water seepage. The powder won't stay dry forever."

Potter and Willcox went on, and about an hour later Pleasants heard from another officer that General Meade had been seen going through the area with General Edward O. C. Ord, now commanding the Eighteenth Corps. At last, Pleasants thought resentfully, the great leader of the Army of the Potomac had deigned to come and look at the mine. But then he realized that Meade's visit most likely was for the purpose of announcing the date set for exploding the mine, and in that case he would be conferring with Burnside, who in due time would pass the word along. So when Meade failed to show up at the mine, Pleasants' disappointment was tempered by his eagerness to learn the time of explosion, and by early afternoon he could contain the suspense no longer. He was about to call on General Potter to inquire for news when he received an order to report to Corps headquarters.

Burnside was pacing back and forth restlessly in his tent like a caged tiger. He answered Pleasants' salute and sat down wearily in his chair. He gave an impression of being utterly tired, but his voice was crisp and forceful.

"Colonel, I had a visit a little while ago from General Meade. He has ordered that the mine be sprung at three-thirty tomorrow morning. I presume you have all in readiness."

"Yes, sir. We spliced those short pieces of fuse, after I sent word back to Headquarters that the longer sections originally requisitioned should be used, if they were obtainable. I understand they are not, so the spliced fuse will have to do. At any rate, that trouble has been taken care of."

"But there is fresh trouble now," Burnside growled. "General Meade has insisted on changing my battle orders at the last minute."

"Good God!" Pleasants burst out. "What do you mean, sir?"

"I mean," Burnside said, "that he has refused to sanction the use of General Ferrero's colored troops in the assault."

"Did he say on what grounds, sir?"

"He insists that they are not sufficiently experienced in combat, and cannot be trusted to do what they are told. He also points out that the Army would be criticized by the public for pushing Negroes into such a dangerous mission, that Northern abolitionist sentiment would accuse us of using the poor blacks for cannon fodder! Can you believe it? Well, apparently General Grant believes it. Meade told me Grant shares his view on this matter entirely. I cannot doubt it; it's no secret that Meade has always been able to influence the General in Chief."

"May I ask what you intend to do now, sir?"

"You may, Pleasants. But I shall not answer you, because I do not know at the moment. My orders are to use white troops. Which ones I have not decided. The choice is up to me, and under the circumstances I can't see that it makes much difference how I choose. Colonel, you've seen those colored men in training?"

"Yes, sir. They looked very good to me."

"They're magnificent. They've been drilling for weeks on one single maneuver. They know exactly what they're supposed to do, and how to do it, and they've got the guts to follow through. I know it. I'd stake my career on them. Now," Burnside looked at his watch, "we've got approximately fourteen hours to go before you touch off that mine. In those fourteen hours I must prepare a white division, one that has had no training for this operation, to make the assault—a division that is below strength and not satisfactorily conditioned."

Burnside's voice was edged with bitterness. Pleasants had never seen him so deeply disturbed before, and he felt a sudden strong bond of sympathy for this man who, scorning the sequestration of rank, did not hesitate to unburden himself as one human being to another. This characteristic, so foreign to many of the higher officers, Pleasants admired and respected.

"If you wish it, sir, my own brigade—"

"Your brigade is exhausted. It will be held entirely in reserve, and will not take part in the assault."

"Then may I ask one favor of you, General Burnside? May I volunteer my services on the staff of General Potter? He has been so enthusiastic over the mine operation that I feel sure he will accomplish whatever is humanly possible."

Burnside considered the proposal for a moment. His eyes measured the figure of this young officer as though appraising him seriously for the first time. Then his stern expression relaxed and the faint trace of a smile softened his features. "Very well, Colonel Pleasants. For tomorrow's action, I shall assign you as provost marshal on my own staff, for duty with General Potter. Now, you must excuse me. Potter and Willcox will be here in a few minutes and we have an important matter to discuss."

Pleasants stood up and saluted. Burnside saluted and extended his hand, and Pleasants took it.

"Thank you, Colonel."

"Thank *you*, sir."

That sultry afternoon, July 29, at the conference in Burnside's tent, there occurred one of those strange lapses of judgment that are an unpredictable element in the functioning of the human machine. Against such uncertainties all efforts in military training are constantly directed. Yet, in times of stress, excusably and inexcusably, with or without precedent, they rise innocently to the surface. If Meade and Grant had erred in tampering with Burnside's original plan, the harassed old warrior was now about to commit a tragic mistake on his own account.

When Willcox and Potter arrived at his headquarters, Burnside told them bluntly that his worst fears had been realized, that Grant had backed up Meade in forbidding the use of the colored troops, and that one of the white divisions would have to be substituted immediately for the attack which would occur tomorrow morning. Both the 2nd and 3rd Division commanders were understandably dismayed and reluctant to commit themselves in any way that might influence Burnside's decision. Before the matter had been discussed at great length, Willcox suggested that the 1st Division commander also be called into conference, and Burnside sent for Brigadier General James H. Ledlie.

It is significant that the Ninth Corps commander did not summon Ledlie until prompted to do so. Clearly it showed a lack of confidence in this officer, who had only recently replaced General Thomas G. Stevenson as leader of the 1st Division. Neither Ledlie's record, nor that of his men, was calculated to inspire confidence. Ledlie himself had had no military training prior to the war, had not distinguished himself on any occasion, and in fact had behaved rather badly in some combat situations. It was said that he was deficient in courage, that he had a weakness for liquor, and that his subordinate officers and men held him in contempt. Burnside may have heard these things; certainly he had not only heard, but seen, that one of Ledlie's brigades was notoriously battle shy. In any case, Ledlie was a man not much to his liking, and he had preferred to discuss his problem only with the two tried and true divisional commanders whom he knew he could trust implicitly, and whose troops were above reproach. But he was fair, and he could not show favoritism.

When Ledlie arrived and was told of the change in plans,

the discussion was begun anew. Willcox agreed that the troops of his own 3rd Division were in the best position to make the advance, but that they had been almost constantly in the line and not as fit as they ought to be. Potter agreed that, next to the 3rd Division, his 2nd Division was in the best attacking position, but he pointed out that his men, too, had been under sporadic fire for a long time and lacked the fresh spirit of combat so desirable in the circumstances. Ledlie readily acknowledged that his own division was less fatigued than either Potter's or Willcox's, but he had little else to say. None of the three generals volunteered for the assignment, and Burnside felt the burden of making the decision resting heavier than ever on his broad shoulders. And the decision could not be put off.

"Gentlemen," he said, "on the strength of your own statements and from my own knowledge of the situation, I find it very difficult to resolve this matter. I want to be fair. Perhaps the only way to be fair is to let chance make the choice. Excuse me for a moment."

He stepped outside the tent, and when he re-entered he held three blades of dry grass in his left hand. Without a word he extended the hand to Willcox, who drew one of the straws. Then Potter drew, and Ledlie, and the three straws were compared. Ledlie had drawn the shortest.

If, at that moment, the Ninth Corps commander felt even the slightest suspicion of having been tricked by fate, his face did not betray it. He shook Ledlie's hand cordially. Then he said: "I am going to send for General Ferrero and tell him what has happened. In the meantime, I want to review briefly some of the details of the plan, so that each of you is completely familiar with them."

When the conference was over, Ledlie was first to leave the headquarters tent. He seemed cheerful, and there was a touch of swagger in his stride. Willcox and Potter followed, their expressions grim. Last came Ferrero, his shoulders slumped, his face slack with dejection.

Alone in his tent, Burnside looked at his watch. It was nearly three-thirty. In twelve hours, Pleasants would light his fuse, the mine would explode, the attack would be on. Looking down, he saw the three blades of dry grass lying on the earthen floor, and with the heel of his boot he ground them gently into the soil.

11

A Terrific Concussion

Against a crimson backdrop painted by the setting sun, the crest of Cemetery Hill showed its formidable silhouette. Beyond it the church spires of Petersburg flashed twilight fire. The sultry day of July 29, 1864, was drawing to its close, and the soft mantle of dusk had already fallen on the big Confederate fort on the slope near the Union lines. When night came on, it was a night like every other night that had come and gone since Grant clamped his siege on the beleaguered city. Streaks of orange flame bespoke the never-ending vigilance of pickets in both camps. Occasional brief bursts of cannonading showed that artillerymen were still alert, if mostly inaccurate. In the thunder of the guns was a dialogue of defiance and braggadocio, often empty and meaningless, but sometimes charged with maiming injury and death. It was a ritualistic exchange of discourtesies that ended the day as appropriately as fireworks end a festival.

Yet this was a very special night. You could sense it, after the pyrotechnics had ceased, in the hot stillness that lay over the whole countryside. There was too much silence. Far back in the Union lines a few campfires gleamed, where the dark-skinned legionaries of General Ferrero sat hunched in mute dejection. Nearer the front, other men were huddled together in darkness, talking in whispers, slithering back and forth in the trenches, checking their gear, trading banter and blasphemy in subdued voices, while their officers hurried to and fro, giving inaudible orders and repeating them in forceful pantomime, all the while looking like creatures earnestly searching for something they would never find.

The three-quarter moon, now high in the sky and showing palely through a heavy veil of cloud, would be low by midnight, Colonel Pleasants noted. By that time much of the confusion of movement quietly boiling around him would have subsided. Now it resembled what he imagined the backstage world of the theater must be like, with a huge company of actors pushing and jostling each other as they readied themselves for the moment when the curtain rises. Perhaps there was a thin theatrical streak in his nature; at any rate, it titillated him to think of the approaching action as an exciting dramatic performance in which he was to play an important part. All this hurrying and scurrying in the trenches, all this scrambling and shoving and frenzied sorting out of troops, was in preparation for the big opening scene of a grim play that he had helped put together. The thought came to him that, no matter how long he lived, no matter how long any man of the thousands here in the Union lines might live, none of them would ever again experience a night exactly like this one.

For a fleeting moment he felt a sudden twinge of compassion for the enemy in the dark fort on the slope. The cards were so pitilessly stacked against them. In his mind's eye he saw the cannoneers of Pegram's battery stretched out on their blankets, their heads pillowed on their arms, sleeping their untroubled sleep in the cradle of a brewing cataclysm. Involuntarily he drew his hand across his face to erase the picture.

For a moment, too, he felt the twinge of apprehension.

There was a chance that the mine might fail to explode. If it did explode, there was a chance that the assault might fail. He had been greatly disturbed by the information passed on to him by General Potter of the lottery at Corps headquarters. How a commanding officer of Burnside's training and experience could have resorted to mere chance in the selection of a leader for so critical an assignment was beyond his comprehension. Ledlie, and Ledlie's division, he considered to be the worst possible choice. And yet, if the powder stayed dry, if the mine exploded properly, the havoc in the Confederate lines would be so great that a brigade of housewives armed with broomsticks should be able to walk into Petersburg.

Feeling better, he groped his way through the ravine and up the slope to the gully where a clump of bushes concealed the entrance to the mine. The two sentries on duty challenged him sharply but in undertones. He gave the countersign and, stooping down, advanced through the low portal to see that the upturned box still shielded the fuse ends. He tapped the toe of his boot against the box, and sat down on it with a sigh.

"Won't be long now, sir," one of the sentries outside said softly.

"No, it won't be long."

. . . Now it was past midnight. The moon had gone down and the sky was black. It was still hot, but a light breeze had sprung up out of nowhere. Campfires had been doused hours before. A single candle glowed dully in the Ninth Corps headquarters tent where Burnside and Ledlie sat at a table with a roughly sketched diagram between them. Burnside was saying: "You understand, General, this thing is going to make a pretty big hole in the ground, and your troops will have to get around it fast to go on up the hill to the crest. . . ."

117

Another candle glowed in Pleasants' tent, where he sat reading and rereading a letter that had come that day from Anne Shaw.

My darling, she wrote, *I have been very anxious and worried about you. You have written to me only once in the past month, and then you had so very little to say! Papa says he thinks something is bound to happen soon at Petersburg, or maybe Richmond, but I am not sure what he means, and I think he is only guessing. If anything is to happen, I hope it may be something good, that will end the war soon. If it is not something good, I trust you will not be involved in it. I pray every night for your safety. . . .*

At a few minutes before three o'clock Pleasants checked his watch, buckled on his saber and pistol, and thrust a small tin box containing a dozen matches in his pocket. At exactly three o'clock he blew out the candle and stepped through the fly of the tent.

It was the hour when all nature seemed fixed in the posture of profound repose. The breeze had disappeared, and there was an ominous stillness in the air. Only a few stars showed in the black bowl of the sky. Not many minutes hence the eastern horizon would yield to the first pale tinge of dawn, but as yet there was no trace of it. Now darkness blanketed everything, and the entire battlefront, where more than a hundred and twenty thousand men were assembled, was as quiet and peaceful as a New England farm.

Pleasants paused for only a moment to accustom his eyes to the darkness, then made his way down the path that led to the ravine. Here, until little more than a week ago, there had been only a dry stream bed, choked with material excavated from the mine, but then the seven-week drought had mercifully ended and now there was water that wetted his boots as he crossed and hurried up the slope toward

118

the gully and the mine entrance. On his left he heard the murmur of voices and the clink of metal, and suddenly he saw the dark outline of massed figures that he knew were Willcox's division, drawn up in readiness to follow Ledlie's troops in the assault. Back of them somewhere was Potter's division. Still farther back, in the trees beyond the old railroad cut, was Ferrero's division—the downcast colored troops whose dream of leading the final great charge that would win freedom for their people had been so rudely shattered at the last moment.

He reached the clump of trees at the mouth of the tunnel, and responded to the low-voiced challenge of the sentries. The guard had been doubled, and two of the men stepped up close and peered intently into his face to make positive identification, then stepped back and saluted. Other figures materialized in the darkness, and Pleasants recognized Captain Hoskings, Lieutenant Douty, and Sergeant Reese. He opened his tin box, struck one of the matches behind his hat, and looked at his watch. It was ten minutes past three.

"Everything ready?" he asked quietly.

"Yes, sir," whispered Captain Hoskings. "I have been in the tunnel as far as the tamping, and stuck my hand through the opening in the sandbags, and along the trough, as far as I could reach. I think the powder is still dry enough to explode."

"You didn't see or hear anything that might indicate the Rebels have discovered the mine?"

"No. Not a thing."

"Thank God for that," murmured Pleasants. "Well, just a few more minutes to go."

As his eyes became adjusted to the darkness, he could see, forward and to the left, the ranks of the 1st Division crowded into the area behind the advanced entrenchments of the Ninth Corps salient. Somewhere up the line a rifle cracked, its echoes reverberating through the ravine, gathering in volume into a low roar as of distant cannon. One of the waiting soldiers had discharged his piece accidentally, and the sound put nerves on edge and spawned an angry growl of curses. Pleasants struck another match. Three-fifteen.

"Let's go!"

The sentries stepped aside and he entered the tunnel, Douty and Reese at his elbow. Douty lifted the wooden box from the fuse ends. Pleasants took a match from the tin container, dropped it, extracted another and scratched it quickly against his side of the box. His hand shook and the flame wavered. Then the fuse sputtered, sizzled—and suddenly with a burst of acrid smoke, the line of glowing fire crept forward toward the pitch-black depths of the gallery.

"I'll give it twenty minutes, boys," he said tersely, checking his watch.

"Half of that, Colonel, if the fuse is any good," Douty whispered hoarsely.

They crawled quickly out of the tunnel as Captain Hoskings came forward, an anxious look on his face.

"The fuse is burning," Pleasants said, and Hoskings nodded with relief. They lingered in tense silence for a minute or two, and then Pleasants mounted the earthwork in front of the trench and stood there, watch in hand.

His reassurance to Hoskings had been given in a whisper, but it might just as well have been shouted through a megaphone. It spread like wildfire, from officer to noncom, from man to man, and a great ripple of excitement passed through the ranks. There was uneasiness, too. For days a rumor had been going around that Army of Potomac Headquarters considered the mine unsafe, had been reluctant to sanction it on the grounds that the explosion might spread destruction through the Union lines, and had finally permitted the project to go on only after a lot of harangue over something that nobody knew anything about—the amount of powder that could be used with reasonable safety.

The rumors were not without some foundation. It was more or less common knowledge that Meade had been strangely uncooperative, and that Pleasants' requisition for powder had been drastically curtailed. Concerning Pleasants, there was a considerable undercurrent of resentment. He was idolized by the men of the 48th Pennsylvania Regiment, well liked by the rest of the troops in his brigade, greatly respected by his fellow officers—even such high-ranking officers as Potter and Burnside. But among the soldiers in divisions outside his own, there were many who mistook his boldness and courage for irresponsibility, and judged him out of hand as a brash young officer who would stop at nothing to get himself noticed in Washington. Maybe he did know something about coal mines, they conceded, but this was different.

And so, while the fuse burned its way deeper and deeper into the tunnel, there was an overlay of apprehension in the wave of excitement that swept through the Union divisions poised for action. After all, who could know exactly what would take place—here in the dark, with all that powder, and the man who had dreamed up the whole crazy idea standing there on the earthwork with his watch in his hand, like Napoleon at Austerlitz. Small wonder that the Irish Catholic lads in Ledlie's division alternately crossed themselves and cursed their luck.

Ten minutes had gone by, and there were growing sounds of restlessness. From the troops massed nearest to him, Pleasants caught the low voices of men fidgeting with impatience. "Gimme a swig from your canteen, Bill." "Where's my damned bayonet?" "Push over, Jed, you're on my feet." "What the hell's keeping us?"

"Silence, men!" came the gruff order from a lieutenant, and the voices subsided.

Minutes passed. It was now three-thirty, and the blast was due at any moment. Pleasants involuntarily braced his stance on the earthwork and riveted his eyes in the direction of the doomed fort. A horse neighed loudly from the cavalry section beyond the hilltop to the rear. Still nothing happened. In the ranks of the 48th Regiment a soldier-miner told his buddy, "This here waitin' around is a hell of a sight harder work than the diggin' ever was."

On the eastern horizon, the blackness of night was turning to gray. Invisible objects were beginning to reveal a suspicion of shape. Now, very dimly, the outline of the Confederate fort could be discerned—and even in outline it appeared ominous and impregnable.

Checking the time, Pleasants noted with dismay that it was a quarter to four! Something was wrong. Perhaps the fuse had gone out. Perhaps the powder was too wet after all, and the whole array of military might, assembled to seize the opportune moment of explosion, would have to be dispersed. Meade would be contemptuous, Burnside laughed at, and he, Pleasants, disgraced! The thought drove him nearly frantic. He jumped down from the earthwork, began pacing nervously back and forth.

Four o'clock. The men in the trenches were becoming noisy again.

Four-ten. It was getting light. In less than an hour the sun would be up.

Four-fifteen. How much longer?

"Men, something has gone wrong." He controlled his voice with an effort. "Either the powder is damp or the fuse is out. I'm going in to see."

He started toward the tunnel, but Douty and Reese were already racing ahead of him. Captain Hoskings laid a hand on his arm. "Stay here, Colonel. Two are enough. Three are too many."

Now the waiting was almost unendurable, and as he stood beside Captain Hoskings every remembered step in the mine operation, from inception to finish, flashed through his mind. The digging. The ventilating. The disposal of earth. The marl stratum. The water seepage. The loading of the magazines. The laying of the fuse.

Sergeant Reese came tumbling out of the tunnel on all fours.

"Give me a knife, somebody. It's the fuse, Colonel. It went out at one of the splicings. We found it. We'll have it fixed." He grabbed the knife and dived back into the hole.

"I knew it," Pleasants rasped through his teeth. "That fuse! All that splicing! Hoskings, sometimes I wonder why the hell . . ."

A messenger came up, breathless from running, and held out a dispatch. In the steadily increasing daylight Pleasants read it without straining.

> "Headquarters Army of the Potomac
> July 30, 1864 4¼ A.M.
>
> Major General Burnside:
> Is there any difficulty in exploding the mine? It is now three quarters of an hour later than that fixed upon for exploding it.
>
> A. A. Humphreys
> Major General and Chief of Staff
> Official   S. Williams
> Asst. Adjt. Genl."

Pleasants tore off a sheet of dispatch paper and scribbled a few words to General Burnside, stating that the fuse had gone out, that it was being repaired, and that the explosion would probably take place very shortly.

The messenger had scarcely gone when Douty and Reese came bursting out of the tunnel. They were covered with mud, choked by fumes, and gasping for breath.

"It's all right, Colonel," Douty panted. "She's burning."

She's burning! She's burning! The whispered word went out again in another rippling wave. Officers and noncoms began excitedly to alert their men, some of whom were doz-

123

ing on their arms. "On your toes, now!" "Stand by to charge!" "I want you fellows to get out of this trench and up that slope on the double!" "Sergeant Berry, wake up that man over there!"

Away back in the Union fortifications, and all along the perimeter of the lines, where great squatting siege guns, mortars, and light artillery fieldpieces pointed their muzzles toward Petersburg, lounging cannoneers waited, lanyards in hand, for the sound that would send them into action.

Pleasants, back again on his earthwork mound, looked at his watch. It was exactly sixteen minutes before five o'clock. The sun would soon be above the horizon. Any moment now. Any moment . . .

"There she goes!"

From the very center of the Rebel earthworks on the slope a solid sheet of flame suddenly shot up, higher and higher, topped by an enormous cloud of gray-black smoke. Like a breath-taking blow to the solar plexus, a terrific concussion of air smote the watchers in the Union lines. The ground trembled violently, and as Pleasants struggled to keep from falling there came a dull grinding roar that grew in volume, swelled to a mighty crescendo, and finally broke away in waves of rolling thunder that lapped and fretted among the hills for a long time before silence swallowed them up.

12

"Where Is Your General?"

In the stunned silence that followed the earth-shaking blast a huge brownish-gray cone billowed up from the hillside in front of the Union entrenchments. High in the sky above it the gray-black plume capping the sheet of flame spread out like a gigantic mushroom. Cone and plume met, merging into one enormous cloud. And suddenly, while the shaken troops watched spellbound, out of the cloud came a horrifying rain of human bodies and debris—splintered timbers, gun barrels and broken mountings, metal and wood in great hunks and tiny fragments, enormous clods of earth, and rocks, and an unidentifiable agglomeration of smashed and shattered miscellany.

With the shock of concussion and the shuddering of the ground beneath their feet, the Union troops had been severely jolted, forced to clutch at each other for support. Then, as the tremor subsided, they stood transfixed by the unleashed fury of the upheaval. Now the cloud of smoke and dust flattened and rolled outward, and in the murky pall that suddenly enveloped them the packed units of the 1st Division were pelted by the fringe fallout from the shower of debris.

Instinctively, this advance line of troops buckled backwards. Some men, panic-stricken, threw themselves flat in the trenches or dived behind breastworks of earth and sandbags. Officers screamed orders and curses, desperately trying to untangle the confused mass and straighten the lines, but not for several long minutes after the frightening eruption had ceased was any semblance of order restored. Half-strangled by the acrid powder fumes, choking and coughing in the dense curtain of dust, the first wave of troops finally moved forward, slowly, blindly, hardly knowing which way to go. Other waves prepared to follow, but encountered unexpected difficulty in getting out of the trenches. The stronger and more agile men clambered out unaided. The less strong and less agile had to be pulled and boosted by sweating noncoms. These front-line trenches were deep, and somehow no one had given much thought to the problem of evacuating them. Sandbags were heaped up to facilitate scaling, ladders were improvised from bayonets thrust into the walls. Men stood on other men's backs and shoulders to climb over the earthworks. Little by little, while the pall of dust and smoke settled ever thicker around them, and confused officers shouted orders that were difficult to understand and sometimes impossible to obey, the bewildered troops of General Ledlie's task force managed to move out in a pattern roughly approximating the paperwork plan.

Over their heads, as they advanced, hurtled the heaviest bombardment of artillery fire the Army of the Potomac had ever laid down. Almost from the instant of the explosion the massed batteries of siege guns, mortars, and fieldpieces began booming into action, their iron throats mocking the spent roar of the mine blast and their hail of metal shredding the enemy lines far back along Cemetery Hill.

Now, after its bumbling start, Ledlie's division was advancing in fairly good order, picking its way cautiously through the dust and the smoke. Colonel Pleasants, mindful of his assignment to the 2nd Division, dashed across the open area from the mine entrance to where General Potter stood waiting at the head of his troops. Willcox's 3rd Division was to follow Ledlie's, the 2nd would advance behind Willcox. Potter's eyes were shining. His muttonchop whiskers seemed to bristle with pride as he grasped Pleasants' hand.

"Colonel, you did it! You did it! It's perfect!"

His throat constricted by emotion, Pleasants could not reply. But the pressure of his handclasp conveyed the respect he had always felt for his commanding officer, and his appreciation of the cooperation he had always received from him. Together, they mounted an earthwork to observe the progress of the attack.

The Second Brigade of the 1st Division had reached the outer fringes of the area where the Confederate fort had stood, and now they were having trouble. This area had been densely obstructed by a broad barricade of felled trees, the branches interlaced to form an almost impenetrable jungle. With the clearing of the air and the improved visibility, it was easy to see that although the fort was gone, most of the barricade remained. The blast had torn only a narrow corridor in the abatis, and through this corridor the assault troops were threading their way cautiously to approach the explosion site.

Here was a serious bottleneck—for as the men reached the spot where the fort had stood they went no farther. Units began crowding together, piling up. Their officers were no longer urging them on. Everyone seemed to be looking down at something that obviously blocked their progress. As the last regiment of Ledlie's division struggled through the abatis, Willcox's division hesitated to follow. Potter focused his field glasses on the scene and then quietly handed the glasses to Pleasants. One quick look told the story.

"General, those troops are completely disorganized! Where in hell is their commander?"

Potter shook his head in despair. "There must be a pretty big hole in the ground. It's got 'em stopped."

"They're supposed to go around it," Pleasants fumed. "No one is leading them. No one is telling them what to do." He looked questioningly at his superior, but Potter shook his head.

"My orders are to follow the 3rd Division," the General said firmly.

"Then I'll go, sir, if you have no objection." And as Potter nodded he dashed away up the slope. Reaching the opening in the abatis he plunged straight through, wondering, as the twigs and branches scratched his face, why Ledlie's men had not been given pioneer equipment to widen this narrow breach. Then he was in the rear of the mass of troops, roughly pushing men aside to force his way through them.

"Move on!" he shouted. "Clear out! Forward!"

And then suddenly he was in the clear, stopped and speechless with the awful sight that met his eyes.

He was on the brink of a crater—a great gaping hole twenty to thirty feet deep, sixty feet wide, and well over two hundred feet long—that had been gouged out of the hillside as if by some giant scoop shovel. Strewn across the bottom of this vast pit was a frightful carnage compounded of human bodies and parts of bodies, twisted pieces of sheet iron, splintered boards and broken beams, dismembered artillery wheels, shattered caissons, ripped canvas covers, and torn blankets. Some of the bodies were writhing, and in the soft earth along the almost vertical sides near the top of the crater he could see figures, half-dead and half-buried, flailing weakly to free themselves. He would remember most vividly, in years to come, the sight of a man without legs, trying to crawl, and a torn-off arm with its hand still grasping a musket whose rope sling entwined the fingers.

They had belonged, he thought, to a cat-napping sentry. Battle conditioned as he was, he felt sick all over. But there was no time to waste, and the sick feeling turned to rage.

"Move on! Get around this thing! Over there to the left, men."

When they stood there, dazed, he drew his saber and struck at them with the flat of the blade.

"Over there! Go around it and on up the hill!"

He grabbed a lieutenant by the arm and shoved him.

"Get your men together! Move out! On the double! On the double!"

He was shouting himself hoarse, striking out with saber and fists like a wild man, and slowly the milling mass of troops began to fan out. Then they did a surprising thing. At a point where the wall of the crater was considerably less than vertical, they began sliding down into it. Some jumped straight from the brink. Unheedful of the orders of a score of officers who had now collected their senses and were trying to save the situation, they went over the edge in droves. Within minutes most of Ledlie's division was wallowing in the crater.

Over the edge, too, went Pleasants. While he shouted and swung his saber he looked in vain for General Ledlie. Perhaps Ledlie knew these troops better, would know how to make them obey. But Ledlie was nowhere in sight. The men were running aimlessly around the bottom of the crater, some of them trying to dig half-buried bodies out of the earth and debris. They were reacting as men react to a natural catastrophe; apparently they had forgotten that this situation was deliberately created to abet a campaign in which they were engaged. It was monstrous, and it was useless.

Pleasants scrambled up the crater wall, found a remnant of the 1st Division trying to get itself organized and to move toward the crest of Cemetery Hill. Again he looked for Ledlie. He asked an excited captain, "Where is your general?"

"Haven't seen him, sir," gasped the captain, turning away to belabor his men.

Down the hill raced Pleasants to General Potter.

"It's no good, sir," he panted. "They're in the crater, most of them, and I can't get 'em out. The whole division is just a mob. Some of the units are actually on the crest, and if we could get the rest up there we'd be all right. But they're just milling around down there in the hole. Sir, can't you take your division up and go around to the right? There's no firing. I think the whole enemy line is paralyzed."

"I'm ready to move out, but my orders are to follow Willcox," Potter said, his voice cool and steady. "His men are coming up through the covered way right now. There won't be room for my division to get through." He paused, compressed his lips. "I'll take a chance on something else."

The chance he took was nothing more than the substitution of common sense for absurdity. An elaborate system of "covered ways" had been constructed—deep trenches roofed over with boards—through which, like cattle going through a chute, the troops of the 2nd and 3rd Divisions were supposed to move through the lines to the front. With Willcox's division now squeezing through these narrow ditches and just beginning to emerge in twos and threes near the foot of the slope, all that Potter proposed to do was by-pass this bottleneck and advance across open ground to a more forward position. He gave some instructions to his chief of staff; in a minute or two the 2nd Division was quickstepping away on a line obliquely to the right. By the time the 3rd Division had funneled through the covered way, both divisions would be ready to press forward around the crater, and a lot of time would have been saved.

But time was running out. Too much of it had been

wasted already, and now the additional quarter of an hour that might have saved the day was not to be had. From a ravine four hundred yards to the left a spattering of musket fire broke the long silence that had cloaked the Confederate lines. It was directed on the remnant of the 1st Division that had just begun to get itself into respectable formation and was starting to skirt the rim of the crater. Men dropped in their tracks under this unexpected attack, and when a concealed Rebel battery opened up a moment later from a grove of trees to the right and dropped a shell squarely in their midst, the remnant broke and scrambled for the nearest cover—over the rim of the crater. Incredibly, most of Ledlie's entire division of more than 3,000 men was now wallowing in aimless confusion in the depths of the big hole.

Bad as this was, the situation soon became far worse. Potter's division made slow progress in its oblique advance, for the terrain was difficult and the slope steep, but the troops were fairly well shielded from fire for the time being. They reached a point near the crater and deep within a line of entrenchments from which the enemy had been routed by the explosion. Here Potter halted his columns. He had exceeded official orders in coming thus far, and he was not disposed to assume any added risk on his own. Had Burnside been anywhere near the front, undoubtedly he would have reversed his original decision and ordered Potter to continue to advance, with Willcox following. But Burnside had set up his battle command post in Morton's Battery, nearly a quarter of a mile back, and Meade was half a mile farther to the rear, at Ninth Corps headquarters. So Potter waited. Finally Willcox's 3rd Division was out of the covered way and crawling up the hill, through the opening in the abatis, toward the crater.

Then the unbelievable happened. These men were tough, battle wise, battle conditioned. Even in the face of growing resistance, with the support of the 2nd Division they could have carried out the objective. But this morning they were short on memory, and the objective was forgotten. Instead of fanning out to the right and left around the crater, as Burnside's original orders stipulated, they plunged straight into it. No doubt their officers had anticipated a shallow, saucerlike depression which would temporarily protect them from enemy fire while providing a short cut to the crest of Cemetery Hill. Why waste time and lives deploying in the open when it could be plainly seen that the thing to do was smash straight ahead? And so the advance units swept over the rim, seeing the thirty-foot drop in front of them too late; and some of the following units charged after them like sheep going over a precipice.

From the commander of the waiting 2nd Division there came a stricken groan of disbelief. "No! Oh, *no!* Pleasants, for heaven's sake, go back and find someone who can straighten out this mess." The muttonchop whiskers and the neatly trimmed mustache flagged his distress, and the voice was no longer calm and steady. "Find Ledlie! Find Willcox! Send a messenger to Burnside, wherever in hell he may be. I'm taking my troops forward. It's getting hot here!"

It was indeed getting hot, for the Rebel battery in the grove of trees to the right had gotten the range and shells were falling all around. Pleasants dashed down the slope, pausing at the bottom to look back. Potter was moving the division around the crater, coming up from behind the shoulder of the hill, and the men were crouched over as they reached the unprotected open area. Pleasants saw the first wave go down under fire, and he took one long breath and dashed on toward the rear. As he ran, leaping across trenches, he wondered whose stupidity was to blame for this sickening sacrifice of his beloved Ninth Corps. Away over on the left was Warren's Fifth Corps, to the right were Ord's Eighteenth Corps and some divisions of Hancock's

Second Corps. Why could not some of these troops be pushed forward? Well, presumably Meade knew what he was doing. This was the kind of thing Meade was equipped to handle, regardless of how little he knew about mines. Anyway, the artillery was giving terrific support. If only they could knock out some of those hidden Rebel batteries.

He came suddenly upon a bombproof, and perhaps because his instincts were especially keen that morning he dived into it. Over in one corner a surgeon was dressing a soldier's wounds. In another corner was Brigadier General James H. Ledlie, sitting on a cracker box and nursing a bottle of brandy. Pleasants drew himself erect and saluted.

"General Ledlie," he said, his voice trembling with suppressed rage, "your division is in complete disorder and the men are huddled in the crater. They are holding up the advance."

Ledlie stared vacantly at him, took a liberal draft from the bottle. "So? I'll 'tend to it. Here, orderly, take this message. Tell those damned regimental commanders to go on, like I told 'em. I've told 'em once. Now I'm telling 'em again. Young upstarts!"

He weaved unsteadily on the box and rolled his eyes. The surgeon in the opposite corner looked up, shrugged a shoulder, and resumed his dressing. Something seemed to snap inside Pleasants' mind. He took a quick step toward Ledlie and shook his fist in the general's face.

"You drunken coward!" he roared. "Take those two stars off your coat and I'll lead your men myself."

Ledlie looked at him dully for a moment. Then his eyes brightened and an expression of craftiness spread over his face. "Can't do it," he muttered. "I'm the division commander. When I tell 'em to go, they go. An' not before. Dam' upstarts!" There was a step outside. "Ah! Here comes ol' Willcox. He'll tell you the same, I bet. Can't get his dam' men out on account of mine, an' I can't get mine out

133

on account of his. Come on, Willcox. Have another drink. I'm going to send another message. Put Bartlett in c'mand. He's up there."

In disgust, Pleasants flung himself out of the bombproof, and on his way to the front met Major J. L. Van Buren, Burnside's aide-de-camp.

"Major, what does General Burnside think of this mess?"

"He's worried, sir. It's pretty bad, isn't it? I've just been up front. That crater is full of men. Some of the Second Corps were ordered forward and they went down in there, too. The worst of it is, the Rebels are rallying all around and they've got us in their field of fire from every angle. Have you seen General Ledlie?"

"He's back there in the bombproof, with Willcox."

Van Buren spat. "That makes three of them, then. General Ferrero is holed up in a bombproof, too. General Burnside wants to send the 4th Division up, and I guess Sigfried and Thomas can handle it. But there'll be hell to pay for this, sir!"

"Never mind," Pleasants said wearily. "If you're going back to the command post, tell Burnside to *do* something—fast!"

He did not know it at the time, but Burnside was having his troubles. Meade was flooding the CP with one dispatch after another. Burnside was to do this. Burnside was to do that. And the Ninth Corps commander, between trying to direct operations from his too-remote position and making excuses for the dereliction of his generals, was nearly beside himself.

Things were worsening at the front. Potter's troops had run into heavy resistance and were being pushed back. Willcox's Second Brigade had been forced to take cover in abandoned enemy trenches on the left of the crater and was pinned down by musket fire. Rebel batteries were still in action, and although Union artillery had silenced some of their guns others were methodically spraying the slope with enfilade fire and dropping shells into the crater. The troops in the crater were now not only trapped, but virtually out of action. Some managed to clamber up the steep sides and fire over the rim, but there were few good targets, and the recoil of their muskets kept dislodging them from their precarious perches. The whole advance had stalled, and everything was at a standstill.

It was now about eight o'clock, and Burnside, drawing on his last resources, ordered his 4th Division forward. With the disgruntled Ferrero missing, Colonels Sigfried and Thomas, the two brigade leaders, took command and shoved their eager troops through the covered ways. Up the slope charged the Negroes with a zest and vigor that, under more favorable circumstances, would quickly have changed the situation. But the Rebel batteries raked them frightfully with grape and canister. At the crater's edge they had no place to go. Colonel Sigfried was determined to keep them out of this cul-de-sac, already teeming with stranded men. He sent them around to the right. Here they ran into the entrenchments of the 17th South Carolina Regiment which had blocked Potter's advance, but instead of bouncing back they obeyed Sigfried's order to charge. Like panthers they tore into the Confederate infantrymen, Thomas's brigade following, and nothing could stop the pent-up savagery of their attack. In the fierce hand-to-hand fighting the enemy trenches were swiftly taken, and though the cost had been considerable the combat spirit of the Negro troops was now honed to razor's edge and they were eager to go on.

From a rifle pit in which he had been forced to take cover, Colonel Pleasants watched the charge of the 4th Division with surging pride and a quick renewal of hope.

Good old Sigfried and his magnificent colored boys had done it! Burnside was right: this was the outfit that should have led the assault. Perhaps they could still save the day!

Two men walked past the rifle pit, completely ignoring the enemy fire still sweeping the hillside. Pleasants was on the point of shouting to them to get under cover when they turned toward him momentarily and he recognized General Grant and his aide, Colonel Horace Porter. There was no mistaking the stocky, bearded figure of the General in Chief. He wore his familiar broad-brimmed felt hat, but he had dispensed with his sword. His coat was an ordinary private soldier's jacket, to the shoulders of which his three silver stars had been carelessly pinned. A long stogie was cocked in the corner of his mouth. Above the stogie the squinting eyes darted quickly from side to side, studying the terrain as coolly as a kibitzer appraising a chessboard.

The general and his aide strolled on, and Pleasants, watching them go unscathed through the rain of fire to another part of the line, wondered what kind of battle this was, with brigadiers in hiding and the Commanding General of the United States Army sauntering nonchalantly along the front, under fire!

Now the colored troops were being formed to attack again, and Pleasants saw Sigfried wave his saber and the black men go out of the captured trenches in a tidal wave of fury. Their objective was the Confederates' second line of entrenchments, specifically the ravine from which most of the harassing musket fire was coming. If this line could be taken and held long enough for the supporting troops of the Fifth and Eighteenth Corps to come up, there was a good chance that the crest could be gained, the trapped units rescued from the crater, and Cemetery Hill taken.

Meade had already ordered the Fifth and the Eighteenth Corps to advance, but General Warren was at this moment consulting with Burnside over the best point to attack, and General Ord was trying with very little success to get around Potter's stranded division which was pinned down and blocking his approach. By the time he had managed to maneuver a clear path, and Warren had cautiously ordered General R. B. Ayres's division forward, the picture had changed hopelessly.

Over in the Confederate lines, behind the crest of the hill, General Robert E. Lee had given calm but decisive orders to General P. G. T. Beauregard, and Beauregard had given orders to Lieutenant General A. P. Hill, and Powell Hill had given orders to Major General William Mahone, and Mahone was stroking his long black beard and preparing to move. This was Mahone the invincible— not much more than five feet tall from the soles of his polished boots to the crown of his gray felt hat, not much more than one hundred twenty-five pounds in weight, and, as General Potter admiringly remarked later, "not much man but a lot of general." Quiet, soft-spoken, immaculate in his plain tent-cloth uniform, he was a dynamo of bold and efficient leadership in the ruthless tactics of infantry warfare. So it was no ordinary resistance that the charging colored troops met as they swept on up to the crest through a furious hail of canister. The solid gray ranks of Confederate defenders that suddenly rose up before them, fixed bayonets gleaming in the sun, were Mahone's men—veterans of the Virginia and Georgia Brigades—infected with Mahone's iron determination.

Bravely the Negro brigades, augmented by miscellaneous white units separated from their own divisions, pressed forward. Some of them reached the gray wall and dented it before being impaled on the bright bayonets. But the Rebel resistance was fantastically desperate, their fire murderous. The charging waves of attackers, black and white, were hurled back. Many of the men tumbled into the crater. The rest, stampeding around it, retreated in wild disorder down the hill.

It was the beginning of the end, and nearly everybody knew it except Burnside. By nine o'clock, Grant's personal inspection of the situation had convinced him further assault was useless, and he told Meade to call off the attack. Meade sent a message to Burnside, but the Ninth Corps commander stubbornly delayed issuing a cease-fire order until he had gone back to headquarters from his command post and argued the matter. Meanwhile, what was left of Willcox's division was driven back to the Union lines. Only Potter's troops were holding on along the right flank of the slope, fairly well protected and still offering some hope for a rally.

Potter had received no orders in a long time. Now, seeing the whole assault crumbling and sensing widespread withdrawal, he sent a message asking permission to make a final attack. Pleasants had rejoined him, and the two crouched down together anxiously and waited for word. When it came, Burnside reluctantly said that he had no discretion in the matter. Peremptory orders for withdrawal had been issued, and this must be done "as soon as practicable and prudent."

Watching Potter's face as he read this message, Pleasants saw the general's lips compress obstinately. Then he said: "Come along, Colonel. I am going to report to General Burnside in person."

They made their way back to the lines, and Potter entered the log-and-sod enclosure that served as the command post. Pleasants, waiting outside, heard heated voices raised in dissension, and then, louder than the rest, the harassed growl of Burnside: "Gentlemen, the order to withdraw is peremptory from General Meade. I am sorry, very sorry. I received this order some hours ago and went to Meade's headquarters. He finally agreed to delay for a while but now he has sent this message. You will act accordingly."

So the last thin strand of hope was snapped. And now the question was not whether Petersburg could be taken, but how long the troops trapped in the crater could hold out against the merciless shelling and the burning heat of the sun. They had used up the water in their canteens, and in the packed masses of the dead, the dying, and the injured, even the able-bodied were exhausted and near suffocation. The withdrawal, first of Willcox's troops and then of Potter's, left them almost utterly defenseless. It was nearly two o'clock in the afternoon when a ragged strip of white muslin knotted to the end of a bayonet was raised above the rim, and the Confederate fire ceased.

13

Leave of Absence

The battle was over, the tables turned. By brilliant leadership and almost superhuman effort General Robert E. Lee and his generals had absorbed the frightful shock of the surprise explosion, had restored order among their panic-stricken troops, had repossessed their abandoned entrenchments while preventing their attackers from swarming through a gap nearly four hundred yards wide. By the irony of fate, they had trapped and slain hundreds of their enemy in the crater which the enemy themselves had gouged.

Moreover, the Confederates had inflicted casualties in a ratio of approximately two to one. Union losses numbered nearly 4,500 dead. The Confederate toll, including an estimated 278 killed outright by the mine explosion, totaled less than 2,500. In every respect the victory was a tragedy, yet for the South it was a victory nonetheless, postponing for nine months the inevitable capture of the besieged city.

There are two sides to every story, and no chronicle of the man-made inferno at Petersburg would be complete without some review of events as they were seen and interpreted by the troops of the Army of Northern Virginia. Unfortunately, there is no record of any official Confederate investigation of the Petersburg episode, hence no official testimony such as was submitted by the principal Union combatants in the subsequent Federal probe. Only from a certain few Rebel participants in the action that day is it possible to obtain a fairly comprehensive picture of what happened, as it appeared from their side of the lines. One of the most articulate and reliable of these eye-witnesses was Captain John C. Featherston, of Lynchburg, Virginia, who served at Petersburg in the famed Alabama Brigade. Long after the war was over, and North and South were reunited, Captain Featherston recalled the explosion of the mine and the Battle of the Crater in public addresses delivered at various patriotic assemblies throughout the East. On one occasion he spoke at Pottsville, Pennsylvania, the home town of Colonel Henry Pleasants and the 48th Pennsylvania Regiment, and if Pleasants could have been present he undoubtedly would have listened to this recital with great interest.

". . . At the time of the explosion, the fort was occupied by Captain Pegram's battery of artillery, with four cannon supported by the 18th and 22nd South Carolina Regiments. The loss of life caused by the explosion of the mine was 256 officers and men of the South Carolina Regiments and two officers and twenty men of the artillery. Two entire companies of the 18th South Carolina Regiment had not a man left to tell the tale. The Confederate troops on each side of the wrecked fort shrank back from this awful explosion, leaving about two hundred yards of our works unoccupied.

"The Federals, anticipating the destructive and demoralizing effect of such a surprise, concentrated a force estimated at 45,000 men near by and in the rear of their works, with which they expected to rush through the opening thus made and capture Petersburg and cut in twain General Lee's army. They then rushed into the crater and adjacent

141

breastworks 12,000 of their infantry, one division of which was composed of Negroes, but, strange to relate, these they hated, which proved fatal to their enterprise."

Captain Featherston was mistaken on this point. However, among the white troops there were elements that held the Negroes in low esteem, and in some instances regarded them with distrust and resentment. Grant and Meade, in rejecting Burnside's proposal to use the colored division as the leading assault troops, undoubtedly took cognizance of this attitude, and leaned over backward to avoid being accused of prejudice at the top-command level. Ironically, in doing so, they condemned the Negro brigades to a worse fate than they would have met in carrying out Burnside's original assignment.

Commenting on the delay in the Union offensive after the explosion of the mine, Featherston said:

"This delay gave General Lee time to prepare to meet the emergency. Anderson's Division of A. P. Hill's Corps was at that time commanded by Major General William C. Mahone. It was the supporting division of Lee's army while in front of Petersburg, and was stationed in the breastworks about three-fourths of a mile to the right of the crater at a point known as the Willcox Farm.

"As soon as General Lee took in the critical condition of affairs, he dispatched one of his staff to General Mahone to send at once two of his brigades to the point of attack. Mahone withdrew the Virginia Brigade, commanded by Colonel Weiseger, and the Georgia Brigade, commanded by Colonel Hall. These two, being on the right of the division, were most accessible and moved by a circuitous route to the scene of action. To have gone direct would have exposed his command to the fire of the entire line of the enemy, which would have meant destruction.

"When General Mahone arrived at a point in front of the crater and was preparing to make his assault, General Lee

142

appeared on the field, mounted on Traveller, his war horse, that by his courage seemed to be conscious of the fact that he bore on his back the fate of a nation."

That General Lee, like General Grant, deemed the situation important enough to require his presence only points up the defection of those lesser leaders in the Union army who, for reasons of personal security or in the mistaken belief that they could maintain better supervision by remote control, remained far back in the lines.

"The Virginia Brigade was placed in the line of battle fronting the captured breastworks on the left of the crater, which was then filling with Yankee soldiers. The Georgia Brigade was filing out of the covered way, preparing to extend the line so as to cover the crater and the works to the right. However, the Virginians noticed that the Union forces were preparing to emerge from the works and charge them. They anticipated this charge and made a dash for the enemy, going into the works and engaging in a hand-to-hand battle, finally recapturing that portion of the Confederate line. The fire of the Union troops was so terrific and deadly that the gallant Georgia Brigade swerved too far to the left, rushing in with and near the Virginia Brigade, after losing nearly or quite all of their field officers and very many of their men. This all occurred by and before 9:30 o'clock A.M."

Despite the superb charges made by these two brigades, and the terrible losses they inflicted on the Union troops in and before the captured trenches, the crater was still occupied, and in a short stretch of entrenchments to the right of it some units of Willcox's 3rd Division were still holding their ground desperately. So General Mahone sent back and ordered up the Alabama Brigade, then commanded by Brigadier General J. C. C. Saunders, under whom Captain Featherston held a company command. Featherston vividly recalled the action.

"As soon as we emerged from the covered way into a ravine or swale running parallel with the works held by the enemy, we there met General Mahone himself on foot. He called the officers to him, explained the situation and gave us orders for the fight.

"He stated that the Virginians and Georgians had by a gallant charge captured the breastworks on their left of the crater, but the enemy still held (the remains of) the fort and a short space of the works to the right of it.

"He ordered us to move our men up the ravine as far as we could walk unseen and then crawl still farther, until we reached a point as near opposite the fort as possible, then order our men to lie down on the ground until the artillery posted in our rear could draw the enemy's fire from a part of their artillery, said to contain fifty pieces, posted on a hill in the rear of their main line. When this was accomplished we should rise up and move at 'trail arms' with guns loaded and bayonets fixed. . . .

"As we were withdrawing from the presence of the General, he said, 'General Lee is watching the result of your charge.'

"We then returned to our men and ordered them to 'load' and 'fix bayonets.' . . .

"According to the morning report, this brigade carried into battle 628 men, practically the same as the Light Brigade which Tennyson immortalized. We walked forward, then crawled, and our guns in the rear soon ceased firing over us. We then knew that the crisis had come.

"The crater was 200 yards distant from where we were lying. By raising our heads we could see the ruined fort and the many flags of the enemy, which indicated their numbers. We knew the odds were greatly against us, but, 'it was not ours to ask the reason why, only ours to do and die.' We knew that we were making General Lee's last

144

play on the checkerboard of war, as we were the last re-
serves.

"Our General gave the command 'Forward' and on we
went. Soon we saw the flash of the sunlight on the enemy's
guns and bayonets as they leveled them over the walls of
the ruined fort. Then a sheet of flame flashed out as they
fired. Then followed the awful roar of battle. This volley
seemed to awaken the demons of hell. It seemed to be the
signal for everybody within range to commence firing. We
raised a yell and made a dash to get under the walls of the
fort before their artillery could open up on us, but in this
we failed. They too joined in the awful din, and the air was
filled with missiles. But on the 600 Alabamians went, as it
seemed literally 'into the jaws of death, into the mouth of
hell.'

"As we reached the walls of the wrecked fort we dropped
on the ground to get the men in order and let them breathe.
As soon as this was accomplished, we pushed up hats on
bayonets, and, as we expected, the enemy riddled them
with bullets, and immediately our men sprang over the
walls and were in the fort. Then commenced that awful
hand-to-hand struggle that history tells you about.

"Whites and Negroes were indiscriminately mixed, and
it was the first time that our troops had encountered the
Negroes, and they could only with difficulty be restrained.

"The work was soon finished. The fort had been reduced
to two compartments. Those in the smaller one cried out
that they would surrender. We told them to come over the
embankment. Two of them started over with their guns in
their hands and were shot and fell back. We heard those
remaining cry, 'They are showing us no quarter; let us sell
our lives as dearly as possible.' We then told them to come
over without their guns, which they did, and all the remainder, about thirty in number, surrendered and were

145

ordered to the rear. In the confusion and their eagerness to get beyond that point, they went across an open field, along the same route over which we charged them. Their artillery, seeing them going to the rear, as we were told, under the flag of truce, thought it was our men repulsed and retreating, and they opened fire on them, killing and wounding quite a number of their own men. One poor fellow, whose arm was shot off just as he started to the rear, said, 'I could bear it better if my own comrades had not done it.'

"This practically ended the fight inside the wrecked fort, but the two armies outside continued firing at this common centre and it seemed to us that the shot and shell rained down from above. They had previously attacked us from below. So this spot was one of the few points of the universe which had been assailed literally from every quarter. The slaughter was fearful. The dead were piled on each other. In one part of the ruined fort I counted eight bodies deep. There were but few wounded compared with the killed."

With all resistance aboveground destroyed, Saunders called for volunteers to seize the crater. Every man in the Alabama Brigade volunteered. It was at this point, however, that the troops trapped in the crater, having reached the limit of endurance and realizing they faced extermination, hoisted their white flag of surrender.

When it was all over, and both sides had counted their prisoners and tallied the damage, Burnside asked for a truce to remove the wounded and bury the dead, but was told that the request would have to come from the general commanding the Army of the Potomac. Meade responded promptly. The truce that followed lasted about four hours, during which the wounded were cared for, and the dead interred three deep in long ditches midway between the lines, while the living of both armies commingled freely and without rancor.

Then the truce expired, the siege was resumed, and once again the troops went under cover and the sharpshooters were back in business.

The Union lines had no sooner settled down to the routine of siege duty than the whole camp became charged with the electricity of bitter recriminations. Ledlie, the commanding general of the 1st Division, whose cowardice and misbehavior had been the direct cause of the failure of his division to go forward, disappeared from view—officially, on sick leave. Willcox and Ferrero remained, but under a cloud. Potter was under some criticism as commander of one of the divisions of the Ninth Corps that had failed in its mission, but it was well known that he had been continuously on the front line and had obeyed orders.

Colonel Pleasants' own feelings were mixed. He knew himself to be perfectly clear of any blame for the fiasco that had occurred. He had completed the mine according to plan, and had exploded it successfully after a delay that actually was more advantageous than otherwise. The effect of the explosion had exceeded his own expectations, for he had had serious misgivings about the reduction in the charge of powder. The fort that barred the approach to Cemetery Hill had been destroyed. An even wider path than had been hoped for had been opened in the enemy lines.

While the attack was being planned he had begged to have an active part in it. After it was launched, he had tried desperately to steer the troops around the crater and to get them out of it after they got in. He had performed several missions under fire, had encouraged General Potter to boldness, tried to shame General Ledlie into doing his duty. And yet the whole project had produced nothing but tragedy, and now he was bitterly disappointed, sick at heart, disillusioned, and resentful.

147

The intense strain of the past three months had begun to tell on him. He was thin, irritable, almost sleepless. Early in the campaign he had been struck on the leg by a piece of rock when a shell exploded near him, and although the bone had not been broken the bruise had been giving him a great deal of pain. More than he knew, he was near the end of his emotional tether, and when his friends in the 48th Pennsylvania Regiment sought him out after the battle to congratulate him on the success of the mine, he came close to bursting into tears.

On Monday, August 1, he received a message to report to General Burnside. He found the Ninth Corps commander sitting alone in his tent, one elbow on a small field desk, his hand supporting his head. Pleasants often recalled in later years that he had never seen a more pathetic picture of remorse, despair, and indignation. Burnside looked years older, and sick, but he acknowledged his visitor's salute with a cordial greeting and sat erect, his brusque, bluff manner slowly returning.

"Colonel Pleasants," he said abruptly, "I have wanted to talk to you privately and personally. First of all I want to congratulate you from the bottom of my heart for the perfect success of your project. It was not your fault that it failed to accomplish what we had hoped for. You did what you did in the face of skepticism and actual interference. The men higher up said it could not be done, and you did it. You have my sincere thanks, which will appear in orders. But I also wanted to thank you personally."

The two had a long conversation during which Burnside frankly admitted his own share of the blame for the fiasco by allowing General Ledlie to command the 1st Division, for not getting order out of chaos, and for having the three division commanders draw lots to determine who would lead the attack after the explosion. Both men were emotionally tense, and Burnside reached into a chest and pro-

148

duced a bottle of brandy and two glasses. The fiery liquor steadied their nerves.

Pleasants listened quietly and sympathetically as Burnside poured out his story of troubles with Meade—how Meade had deluged him with dispatches, hour after hour, all through the battle; how he had finally been stung into retaliating with a caustic message that was sure to be construed as insubordination; how Meade had given him a peremptory order to withdraw his troops while he, Burnside, felt there was still a chance to gain the objective of Cemetery Hill. He seemed to obtain some comfort in going over the sheaf of dispatches that had been showered upon him at a time when he was beside himself with anxiety and responsibility. He told Colonel Pleasants that General Meade probably would prefer charges against him. Also, there would be an investigation that would undoubtedly require the testimony of all officers concerned with the mine and the subsequent fiasco. Pleasants, of course, agreed to be of any help he could. He explained, however, that he was now so exhausted and sick that he would like to apply for a short leave of absence to collect his senses and get some rest. This General Burnside cheerfully agreed to endorse to General Meade.

Two days later, Meade sent for Pleasants, and Pleasants rode over to the commanding general's headquarters, three miles south of the Ninth Corps salient. He was ushered into an atmosphere of cold formality that contrasted strangely with lesser headquarters he had visited. The pervading sense of neatness and precision gave him the fleeting impression that the very grass blades under the General's feet were combed regularly each morning. Meade rose deliberately from a camp chair, acknowledged the salute, and held out his hand. Pleasants took it diffidently, and Meade stood towering above him—a great, bearded, imposing figure in his faultlessly tailored uniform. His high cavalry boots with extra tops were brilliantly shined, his brass buttons and trappings dazzlingly bright. His eyes, deep-set beneath a high, well-molded forehead, were heavily lidded like those of a thinker, but in their gray depths Pleasants thought he detected a quick flash of cunning—the cool, calculating avariciousness of a clever aristocrat. The voice was low and suave.

"Colonel Pleasants, I wish to congratulate you on the success of your project. The mine was entirely satisfactory from a military standpoint, and you deserve great credit. I have had orders published to that effect. If the attack following the explosion had not been so badly bungled, the whole affair would have been a very considerable victory. Will you have a glass of Madeira?"

"Thank you, no, General Meade." Pleasants was remembering the difficulty he had had in obtaining a theodolite, the delay in supplying the powder, the short pieces of fuse that had had to be spliced, the score of ways in which this man had seemingly sought to frustrate and embarrass him.

"Colonel Pleasants, you have applied for a leave of absence, I believe, endorsed by General Burnside."

"Yes, sir."

"Well, I am glad to give my approval. There is an investigation pending, but I do not think it will require your testimony. Your leave is granted."

"Thank you, General Meade." Pleasants saluted and walked out of the tent.

Papers confirming a ten-day leave of absence were forwarded to him next day, and he made preparations to go by boat to Baltimore, en route to Philadelphia. He had seriously considered a trip to Lexington to visit Anne Shaw, but the prospect of the long and tiresome journey, the necessarily short stay, and the pang of parting again from the girl of his dreams were discouraging. His term of service would expire in mid-December, and he decided to postpone a reunion with Anne until his military career was behind him and he could plan, with her, for their future together. Meanwhile Uncle Henry and Aunt Emily were anxiously waiting to see him, and the vision of quiet old Rockland, with its serenity and shade, welled up in his memory as an irresistible sanctuary from the hell he had endured.

The old home was even more precious in its reality than it had seemed in memory when he dismounted wearily from the dusty train at Morgan's Corner (now Radnor, Pennsylvania) and climbed into the buggy beside his Uncle Henry. He could scarcely contain his feelings during the poky ride from the station behind the shaggy old horse, and when at last he saw from the top of the last hill the white walls and hospitable "upper and lower" porches of Rockland, he felt the weight of his troubles lifted.

There was a long and tearful embrace from his Aunt Emily awaiting him. There was also a freshly arrived letter from Anne, its firmly rounded lines flowing happily across the paper in sentences bursting with pride. She longed to see him, but he was wiser, she said, to have deferred coming to Lexington—"because the whole city would have mauled the hero to death!"

Back at the Headquarters of the Army of the Potomac, the hero had been paid a more restrained tribute. Captioned General Orders No. 32, under date of August 3, 1864, it had been issued too late for him to see before going on leave. It read as follows:

> The Commanding General takes great pleasure in acknowledging the valuable services rendered by Lieut. Col. *Henry Pleasants,* 48th Regiment Pennsylvania Veteran Volunteers, and the officers and men of his command, in the excavation of the mine which was successfully exploded on the morning of the 30th ultimo under one of the enemy's batteries in front of

the Second Division of the Ninth Army Corps. The skill displayed in the laying out of and construction of the mine reflects great credit upon Lieut. Col. *Pleasants*, the officer in charge, and the willing endurance by the officers and men of the regiment of the extraordinary labor and fatigue involved in the prosecution of the work to completion are worthy of the highest praise.

By command of Major General Meade:

S. WILLIAMS, *Assistant Adjutant General*

Meade had kept his word, confirming by official record his verbal acknowledgment of services rendered in construction of the mine. It was a belated gesture. It may or may not have been made in genuine sincerity. In any case, the commanding general was undoubtedly relieved by Pleasants' departure. The investigation was coming, and it was just as well to have this fiery and embittered young man miles away from the proceedings.

14

The Last Encounter

Few military engagements in all history can compare with the Battle of the Crater. From start to finish it is a study in crises and contrasts, beginning with the extraordinary success of the Union army in excavating a tunnel of unprecedented length and effectively setting off a mine blast, and ending with dismal failure and appalling loss of life. In between these extremes of success and failure were crowded events that reflected their own extremes of brilliant leadership and colossal blundering, heroism and cowardice, timidity and aggressiveness, sound judgment and inexcusable error, generosity and selfishness, humility and conceit, noble impartiality and petty jealousy, love and hate, prudence and stupidity. All these and more were stirred in the hot cauldron of combat on that hot July morning—and what came to the surface was tragedy.

Paradoxically, in the midst of many explanations, the tragedy was inexplicable. Everyone could ascribe a reason, and none of the reasons was satisfactory. Throughout both North and South the news was shocking and puzzling. The man in the street was unable to understand what had happened, and the newspaper he read didn't give much help. The whole thing made no more sense to the citizens of New York and Boston than it did to the citizens of Raleigh and Savannah. And in Washington, as in Richmond, there were not enough answers to go around. An investigation was inevitable. General George G. Meade knew it, and took the initiative.

Even before Colonel Pleasants was safely out of the way, Meade had applied to President Lincoln to order a court of inquiry. Lincoln promptly directed Secretary of War Edwin M. Stanton to issue the order, dated August 3, which named Major General Winfield S. Hancock, Brigadier General Romeyn B. Ayres, Brigadier General Nelson A. Miles, and Colonel Edward Schriver as the court detail, "to examine into and report upon the facts and circumstances attending the unsuccessful assault on the enemy's position on the 30th of July, 1864." Hancock served as president of the court, Schriver as inspector general and judge advocate. Hancock's own Second Corps headquarters was used as the courtroom, and it was there that all sessions of the inquiry were held, starting Saturday, August 6, one week after the Battle of the Crater, and continuing to September 9.

The first testimony was taken on Monday morning, August 8, and the first to testify was Meade. Neatly and precisely he summarized the events leading up to the explosion of the mine, described his impressions of the assault, and read the long succession of dispatches sent and received by him during the action. He concluded by saying that he had no desire to direct censure on anyone for his army's "unfortunate failure"; that, as a matter of fact, he had not yet been given sufficient information by General Burnside and his brigadiers to enable him to censure anyone. He was careful to emphasize that Burnside had not yet submitted an official report, and to imply that the Ninth Corps commander had been deliberately uncooperative in intelligence matters.

"I have very little knowledge of what actually transpired except from the dispatches you have heard read here," he said. "I have been groping in the dark since the commencement of the attack. I did not wish to take any unpleasant measures, but I thought it my duty to suggest to the President of the United States that this matter should be investigated, and that the censure should be made to rest upon those who are entitled to it. What I have done has been to show that I tried to do all I could to insure success."

For a man who professed to know so little of what had happened, Meade took up a surprising amount of the court's time, and for one who had no desire to point the finger of blame he did a pretty good job of indicating where the finger should be pointed. Cleverly enough, in thus setting the stage for the inquisition he eliminated himself, to a considerable degree, from any suspicion of blame.

General Burnside followed Meade on the stand. For three straight days—days that must have been as trying to him as any in his military experience—the doughty old warrior told his story in complete detail. He defended himself on the intelligence issue, saying that he had replied to all dispatches from Meade as best he could, although candidly admitting that one of his replies had been insubordinate. He defended the conduct of his troops, and said he did not know of a single order that had not been carried out by his division commanders. He excused General Ledlie as being "very sick, not able to stand the oppressive heat" on the day of the battle. In answer to a question, he said he believed the 4th Division "would have made a more impetuous and successful assault" than the 1st Division made.

The inquiry dragged on and on. Before it was over, every officer of consequence who had been involved in the episode had a chance to say his say—Potter, Ferrero, Willcox, Ord, even General Grant himself. In all, Hancock's court listened to the testimony of thirty-two persons during sixteen days in session. On September 9, the seventeenth and final day, it reported its findings and rendered an opinion.

There were four reasons, the court said, why the assault

155

should have been successful: (1) the surprise of the explosion, (2) the comparatively small force in the enemy's works, (3) the enemy's ineffective fire, and (4) the fact that some of the Union troops had been able to advance as much as 200 yards beyond the crater, toward the crest of Cemetery Hill.

But the assault failed, the court found, for these reasons: (1) injudicious formation of the troops, and their advance by flank movement rather than by extended front, (2) the halting of the troops in the crater, (3) no proper employment of engineer officers and working parties, and of materials and tools for their use, in the Ninth Corps, (4) poor leadership of some of the units in the assault columns, and (5) the want of a competent common head at the scene of the assault.

In its opinion, the court said, the evidence appeared to show that General Burnside, General Ledlie, General Ferrero, General Willcox, and Colonel Z. R. Bliss, commanding the Second Brigade of Potter's Division, were "answerable for the want of success which should have resulted."

The conclusions arrived at by the court came as no particular surprise to anyone. Colonel Pleasants, who had returned to duty long before the proceedings came to an end, reflected bitterly that the spit-and-polish generals had at last succeeded in nailing Burnside's hide to the wall. The old warrior was soon removed from command of the Ninth Corps. General Ledlie was permitted to resign.

There was still a war on. Having boiled over madly in the Battle of the Crater, it now simmered down again to a state of siege. But it was still a war—a campaign of slow attrition that wore terribly on the nerves of officers and men. From time to time, as summer yielded to autumn, there were active engagements. One of these, on September 30, took place when an effort was being made to extend the Union lines farther around the enemy's right flank to a position known as Poplar Springs Church.

Some Ninth Corps units were involved in this action, including the 48th Pennsylvania Regiment. A week later Pleasants was commissioned a full colonel, having earlier declined the commission of Brevet Colonel of Volunteers. On October 27, in an unsuccessful Union attack against Confederate entrenchments at Hatcher's Run, he fought his last important engagement of the war.

Early in December the 48th Pennsylvania, along with the Seventh Rhode Island Regiment and two batteries of artillery, was transferred to the occupation of Fort Sedgwick, on the edge of the Jerusalem Plank Road immediately in front of Petersburg. This post, so near the Rebel lines and under such constant fire that the soldiers dubbed it "Fort Hell," was put in Colonel Pleasants' charge, and it was here that his military career came to an end.

He was due to be mustered out of the service on December 18. On that day, to reach the tent of the commanding officer who would issue his discharge, it was necessary to pass within the line of enemy fire. Far from feeling any trepidation, Pleasants contemplated this hazard with grim satisfaction. By his own peculiar standards of reasoning the situation seemed right and proper. He had entered the army with almost suicidal intent, expecting if not actually hoping that somewhere along the line in his career of service he would be killed in action. True, as the sharp edges of his own personal tragedy were dulled by time, and a woman's love reawakened a love of life, his attitude had changed. Yet he had never avoided danger for its own sake and he was not disposed to do so now. His life had been spared for nearly four long years. Therefore it would seem that he was destined to survive, and if so he had nothing to fear. In any event, for the morale of the officers and men around him who still had many months to serve, it was imperative to retire with all the flags of his courageous spirit flying.

Deliberately, unhurriedly, he left the fort, walking across the open space toward the Jerusalem Plank Road for nearly a hundred yards in full view of the enemy, while his own men watched with bated breath. Rebel sharpshooters blazed away eagerly at this astonishing target, and the bullets whined around him, but he was untouched. When he had received his discharge papers and tucked them carefully in his pocket, he returned to his quarters—but this time he chose the most protected route he could find.

Now it was time to bid farewell to his old command. Down in the depths of the bombproof the officers and men were assembled. Behind the mud-spattered figures in that gloomy, candle-lit cavern stood the frayed colors that had been carried through so many battles. Standing beside his old friend, Lieutenant Colonel George W. Gowen, to whom he was to turn over command of the 48th, Pleasants carefully scanned the group. He could recognize only a pitiful few of those who had gone out with him from Pottsville in '61. Most of the old guard had been killed, wounded, or captured. Seeing so many new faces, yet knowing that the regiment's *esprit de corps* had not changed, he marveled for a moment at the unfailing truth that men first mold military units, and then the units mold men.

Two sergeants from Companies A and E lifted tattered banners and brought them forward. Silence filled the room. Pleasants cleared his throat.

"Men of the 48th," he said quietly, "I am leaving you. You have served me loyally and well. We have gone far, and have seen much together. I can never express my thanks to you for your faithful devotion. It was through no fault of yours that this bitter war did not end on the thirtieth of last July. It was the decree of fate. I am turning over to my loyal, brave and efficient right-hand officer, Lieu-

158

tenant Colonel George W. Gowen, these colors which have been carried so far, so successfully. May you serve Colonel Gowen as you have served me and your flag. And may God bless you, boys, and bring you and the colors safe home. Farewell."

He turned the colors over to Gowen and shook hands. Then, with a wave of the arm, his lips quivering in a sad smile, he walked steadily up and out of the dugout.

It was the week before Christmas and he was on his way to Lexington, cheered by the prospect of spending the holiday season with Anne yet vaguely disturbed and dejected by the broken ties of his military service. Everywhere he went, on the train and at station stops along the way, people were saying that the war was surely drawing to a close, that the backbone of the Confederacy was broken, and by winter's end there would be peace and the restoration of national unity. Asked for his opinion, he could give none. His perspective was unclear; he had been too much in the forest to be able to see the trees.

Hospitable Lexington was unchanged and warmly vociferous in its welcome. Anne, bright-eyed, more mature, and more lovable than ever, received the grave stranger with tender, passionate longing. He responded slowly to these mellowing influences. So much had happened since those faraway days when he had served as the city's provost marshal. There was so much to think about, talk about— and for a long time he would think too much and talk too little. But old friends in Lexington outdid themselves to make him forget the troubles and anxieties he had undergone. There were gay parties, a memorable Christmas dinner in Hiram Shaw's magnificent home, and best of all a New Year's Eve with Anne that magically inspired a sudden overwhelming rush of shared plans and confidences.

When he left Lexington early in January, 1865, the shape

of the future was clearly defined at last. It was a future which most certainly included his marriage to Anne, but because she was not yet eighteen and he was nearly thirty-two, the marriage would be postponed until he had found a job, saved up some money, and become fully adjusted to the workaday world of civilian life again. With rare common sense that matched her beauty, Anne Shaw concurred in this decision.

He returned to Rockland, and after a brief rest got in touch with the Philadelphia and Reading Coal and Iron Company at Pottsville regarding possible employment. Promptly the company notified him that it would be glad to have his services in exploring the possibilities for development of its extensive lands. Just as promptly, Pleasants decided to accept.

But the same mail had brought another letter—an important message from Washington. His presence, the letter said, was desired immediately in connection with a Congressional investigation of the failure of the attack on Petersburg. He left for Washington next day.

The Congressional investigation had been going on for three weeks or more. On December 15, Senator Henry Bowen Anthony of Rhode Island had introduced a motion in the Senate of the United States, stipulating that the Joint Committee on the Conduct of the War be directed "to inquire into and report the facts concerning the attack on Petersburg, on the 30th day of July, 1864." The motion came logically from Mr. Anthony; he was a former editor of the *Providence Journal,* and he had a newspaperman's inquiring mind. Two days later, December 17, the probe was on and General Burnside was going all over the whole sad story again. Testimony taken during the earlier military court of inquiry was reviewed and compared, and again the endless flow of dispatches was examined. A few days before

Christmas the Joint Committee had adjourned its sessions in Washington and gone directly to the Union lines at Petersburg to hear the direct testimony of the officers who were then too busy fighting a war to leave the area. Then the investigation was carried back to Washington again, and there, on January 13, Colonel Pleasants went to the stand.

He welcomed the opportunity. In no uncertain terms he recounted the details of constructing the mine, stressed the cooperation he had received from Burnside and the lack of cooperation he had received from the Headquarters of the Army of the Potomac. The powder, the fuses, all the makeshift paraphernalia that had been used in digging the tunnel, were penetratingly discussed in questions and answers. He was gloomily convinced that all this talk would accomplish nothing, but there was satisfaction in releasing some of the feeling of injustice that had been so long bottled up within him.

Inevitably he was asked what he considered to be the cause of the failure of the assault.

"I have thought of that a great deal," he said. "There were several causes for the failure. The first and immediate one was the failure of the First Division of the Ninth Corps to go beyond the enemy's works. The whole of them, or a great portion of them, went up very promptly and occupied the enemy's works. There was nothing to resist them. But they remained there and did not go beyond. When the other divisons came up, they were all mixed up. They were all in a medley. That was the immediate reason of the failure."

A more remote reason, he said, was that the troops were massed too far back, but that General Burnside had done this only because he feared there might be injuries caused by the explosion.

By the time the Joint Committee completed its investigation four days later, a total of fourteen witnesses had been heard, and almost as many different viewpoints and opinions had been derived. Over and over again the question had been asked: To what do you attribute the failure of the attack?

Burnside attributed it to the last-minute change in his plan to have the colored troops lead the attack, and to the lack of participation by the Fifth and Eighteenth Corps.

Meade blamed everything on delay and bad timing in carrying out orders, even going so far as to say that the delay in springing the mine had been a contributing factor. Here he came close to blaming his own headquarters, since the cause of that delay certainly originated there.

Generals Willcox and Potter backed up Burnside by criticizing the lack of active support from Warren's and Ord's corps, while Warren himself blamed the narrow covered ways for having created a bottleneck and the Ninth Corps commander's lack of foresight in not having more of the abatis cleared away. On the latter point, Major Duane readily concurred, while Burnside protested that the abatis was no great obstruction.

General Ferrero blamed the 1st Division for not having gone forward and around the crater, but added that it was his opinion the assault should not have been aimed at the crater in the first place; instead, it should have been directed "a little to the left."

General Grant, in his slow but characteristically complete and comprehensive manner, had given his questioners an unbiased picture of the whole affair, even to blaming himself.

"I blame myself a little for one thing," he said. "I was informed of this fact: that General Burnside, who was fully alive to the importance of this thing, trusted to the pulling of straws which division should lead. It happened to fall on what I thought was the worst commander in his corps.

I knew that fact before the mine was exploded, but did nothing in regard to it. That is the only thing I blame myself for. I knew the man was the one that I considered the poorest division commander that General Burnside had. I mean General Ledlie."

Earlier in his testimony Grant had said: "General Burnside wanted to put his colored division in front, and I believe, if he had done so, it would have been a success."

Thus were submitted, reviewed, and weighed the observations and judgments of some of the Union army's highest officers, as well as others of lesser rank. One and all, they were men trained to observe and judge military operations. Each had seen what had happened, with his own eyes. Perhaps, in interpreting what he had seen, each one, knowingly or unknowingly, mixed fact with fancy, truth with error. Out of the welter of words there emerged, little by little, the picture that General Meade so obviously intended to create—the picture of incompetence in Ninth Corps leadership. It was the same picture that had emerged at the military court of inquiry, but now it was being studied by men of a different breed, in an atmosphere far removed from the scene of battle, and after an interval of time in which impressions had jelled to a firmer consistency. It was being studied painstakingly, with meticulous care, in order to arrive at just and unbiased conclusions. And so there was a surprise in store.

On January 17, four days after Pleasants appeared to testify, the Joint Committee terminated its investigation, and its chairman, B. F. Wade, subsequently issued a lengthy report. The last two paragraphs of that report are of special significance:

> "Your Committee desire to say that, in the statement
> of facts and conclusions which they present in their

report, they wish to be distinctly understood as in no degree censuring the conduct of the troops engaged in this assault. While they confidently believe that the selection of the division of colored troops by General Burnside to lead the assault was, under the circumstances, the best that could have been made, they do not intend thereby to have it inferred that the white troops of the Ninth Corps are behind any troops in the service in those qualities which have placed our volunteer troops before the world as equal, if not superior to any known to modern warfare. The services performed by the Ninth Corps on many a well-fought battlefield, not only in this campaign but in others, have been such as to prove that they are second to none in the service. Your Committee believe that any other troops exposed to the same influences under the same circumstances, and for the same length of time, would have been similarly affected. No one, upon careful consideration of all circumstances, can be surprised that those influences should have produced the effects they did upon them.

In conclusion, they, your Committee, must say that, in their opinion, the cause of the disastrous result of the assault of the 30th of July last is mainly attributable to the fact that the plans and suggestions of the general who had devoted his attention for so long a time to the subject, who had carried out to a successful completion the project of mining the enemy's works, and who had carefully selected and drilled his troops for the purpose of securing whatever advantages might be attainable from the explosion of the mine, should have been so entirely disregarded by a general who had evinced no faith in the successful prosecution of that work, had aided it by no countenance or open approval, and had assumed the entire direction and control only when it was completed, and the time had come for reaping any advantages that might be derived from it."

In this report Colonel Pleasants' recorded testimony was the first to be cited, indicating that the Joint Committee had considered it of prime importance and had been strongly influenced by it in arriving at its conclusions. There was a peculiar satisfaction in this for the young man now free to return home and attend to his own personal affairs.

Suddenly, for him, everything was crystal clear and the future was bright. Petersburg would fall but it would rise again. The Confederacy would die, but the spirit that had kept it alive would be transmuted into the upbuilding of one great nation, and live on in a glorious unity of human endeavor. The South would be beaten down, but it would emerge like a phoenix from its ashes, stronger than before.

So let the controversy go on. Let historians argue and future generations continue to seek for the answers that had already been written in blood. He had done his best and he had told the truth—and he had come to believe that, in war as in peace, no worthy effort is wasted and no grain of truth lost.

Epilogue

On April 9, 1866, President Andrew Johnson signed the commission that made Henry Pleasants a Brigadier General by Brevet, "to rank as such from the thirteenth day of March in the year of our Lord one thousand eight hundred and sixty-five, for skilful and distinguished services during the war, and particularly for the construction and explosion of the mine before Petersburg, Virginia."

His marriage to Anne Shaw took place the following year. They made their home in Pottsville, Pennsylvania, where he had gone to work for the Philadelphia and Reading Coal and Iron Company. In 1870 the company promoted him to chief engineer. A spectacular demand for anthracite coal for use in industry was just beginning, and for three years General Pleasants rode the crest of the tidal wave to prosperity.

In 1873 he was made general superintendent of the Coal and Iron Police, and became deeply involved in the fight to stamp out a secret organization of coal region terrorists known as the "Molly Maguires," who were fast gaining a strangle hold on the mining industry. How General Pleasants and his police, aided by Pinkerton detectives and a few fearless citizens, broke up the organization and brought its ringleaders to justice is one of the thrilling epics of the 1870's in America, particularly noteworthy for the fact that this crusade against lawlessness and gangsterism restored the faith of the people in the wisdom, integrity, and courage of their officials and their courts. However, that story has no place here.

In June, 1873, shortly before he was to begin his strenuous campaign against the "Mollies," General Pleasants was vacationing at a celebrated hotel in Cape May, New Jersey, with his wife and their three young children. One day, in the dining room where they were at dinner, an excited buzz of conversation spread among the guests and Pleasants looked up to see the President of the United States entering the room. It was Ulysses S. Grant, in person, accompanied by several members of his cabinet and a brace of army officers.

Pleasants had never quite forgiven Grant for his lack of interest in the mine, and for his Meade-can-do-no-wrong attitude, and he resolved to avoid recognition if possible. But after a while he became aware that Grant was looking hard in his direction. Then, covertly, he saw the President lean toward one of his staff and ask a question, nodding his head in his direction. Presently one of the officers arose and approached the Pleasants' table.

"Excuse me, sir. Are you General Pleasants?"

"I am, sir."

"President Grant presents his compliments and asks that, if it is convenient to you, you will please come to his parlor after dinner."

Pleasants nodded. Later, when the distinguished guests had finished their meal and left the room, he asked to be shown up to the Presidential suite, tapped on the door, and was immediately ushered into the room where Grant was stretched out in a chair, coat carelessly unbuttoned, and the inevitable black cigar between his teeth. He rose at the announcement of his visitor's name and came forward, hand extended.

167

"General Pleasants, I have tried to meet you personally many times. I know that you left the army with harsh feelings for which I was as responsible as anyone. I have asked you to do me the honor of coming here today in order that I may express to you the regret I have always felt in the failure of your magnificent project. It was no fault of yours, and I am only sincerely pleased that the Senate saw fit to honor you with the brevet of brigadier general after you left the service. It was little enough for them to do. I do want to congratulate you, even at this late date."

When Pleasants left the suite after an hour of delightful reminiscence, his estimation of Grant had altered tremendously. He was convinced that at heart the President was kind, generous, honest, and faithful, and that his personal failings and the errors attributed to him during his administration resulted largely from the web of political intrigue that had been spun around him. He began to see that Grant had been caught in this web and dominated in the same way that he had been overawed and compromised during the war by the suave and clever aristocrat who commanded the Army of the Potomac.

It was in the latter part of that good decade, the seventies, that General Pleasants reaped the real bounty of well-being. He was in his mid-forties—handsome, successful, prosperous, with a potentially long and useful career still before him in a rewarding industry. Anne, not yet thirty, was a radiantly beautiful and devoted wife and mother, and the three children she had given him—Emma, John, and James—were healthy, promising youngsters. These, the seventies, were the halcyon years of his life. Wisely, he enjoyed them to the full, for tragedy was on the way once more.

He began to suffer excruciating pains in his head. Doctors attributed the pains to nervous strain, urged him to take frequent long periods of rest. But the pains persisted—blinding, burning headaches that gradually became almost unendurable. Toward the close of that decade, while he and Anne were traveling in Europe, he consulted the famous French nerve specialist, Professor Charles Edouard Brown-Sequard, at the College de France. The shock came when the great man bluntly told him that he was suffering from an inoperable brain tumor.

The diagnosis proved to be correct, but General Pleasants calmly continued his trip through Europe, fighting the staggering pains, keeping the secret of his doom locked inside him, heaping lavish gifts on the lovely wife who did not yet sense the gravity of his illness. In Brussels he bought for Anne a five-hundred-dollar black silk shawl. Then he returned home to await the inevitable.

His death, on March 26, 1880, at the age of 47, came as a blessed release from suffering. Yet tragically, it came too soon, for only a few months later medical science perfected a means of surgery that might easily have spared him for several more useful years. But it was too late. Like the spliced fuse in the Petersburg mine, the sputtering spark of his life had gone out, and there was no one to relight it.

At Pottsville, Pennsylvania, among the Schuylkill County hills and hearts he loved, he was laid to rest in the Episcopal faith that he had embraced as a child at old St. David's Church in Radnor. A modest stone marks his grave, but his real monument endures in a curious depression in the ground on a hill outside Petersburg, Virginia.

This is symbolic, for it would seem that fate had early charted Henry Pleasants' course among the peaks and valleys of life, so that he was unalterably committed to the extremes of height and depth, accomplishment and frustration, success and disappointment, bliss and misery.

Perhaps, since plateaus are reserved for timid men, no other road would have been tolerable to his impetuous nature.

Bibliography

Abbott, John S. C.: *History of the Civil War in America,* H. Bill, New York, 1866.

Army Regulations, Harper, New York, 1861.

Beauregard, P. G. T.: *Four Days' Battle at Petersburg, Battles and Leaders of the Civil War,* Century, New York, 1884–88.

Bishop, Carter R.: *Letters Re Crater Battlefield and Museum.*

Bosbyshell, Oliver C.: *The 48th in the War,* Avil, Philadelphia, 1895.

Catton, Bruce: *A Stillness at Appomattox,* Doubleday, New York, 1954.

Churchill, Winston S.: *History of the English-Speaking Peoples,* vol. 4: *Great Democracies,* Dodd, Mead, New York, 1956-1958.

Civil War Round Table: *News Letter,* Vol. 4, No. 9, Nov. 24, 1954.

Civil War Round Table: *Letters Re Address from Officials,* etc.

Colston, R. E.: *Repelling the First Attack on Petersburg, Battles and Leaders of the Civil War,* Vol. IV, p. 535, Century, New York, 1884–88.

Creason, Joe: *Politics of Kentucky,* etc., *Civil War Times,* Box 1861, Mechanicsburg, Pennsylvania.

Featherston, John C.: Address, *Battle of the Crater,* Pottsville, Pennsylvania, Apr. 18, 1906.

Funk and Wagnalls Encyclopedia, 1952.

Gilham, William: *Manual of Instruction for Volunteers and Militia,* Charles Desilver, Philadelphia, 1861.

Gondos, Victor: Correspondence War Records Office, National Archives, Washington.

Gould, Joseph: *The Story of the 48th,* Slocum, Philadelphia, 1908.

Grant, Ulysses S.: *Personal Memoirs,* Webster, New York, 1892.

Grant, Ulysses S.: *Report of Armies of the U. S., 1864–1865* (Official Copy).

Hale, Wesley: Correspondence Re Crater Battlefield Restoration and Notes.

Hanson, Joseph Mills: *A Stolen March: Cold Harbor to Petersburg, Journal of the American Military History Foundation,* Washington, D. C., Vol. I, No. 4, Winter 1937–38.

Hergesheimer, Joseph: *Sheridan, A Military Narrative,* Houghton Mifflin, Boston, 1931.

Houghton, Charles H.: *In the Crater, Battles and Leaders of the Civil War,* Vol. IV, p. 561, Century, New York, 1884–88.

Humphreys, A. A.: *The Virginia Campaign—1864,* originally published 1883, reissued by The Blue & The Gray Press, New York.

Kautz, August V.: *Operations South of the James River, Battles and Leaders of the Civil War,* Vol. IV, p. 533, Century, New York, 1884–88.

Kilmer, George L.: *The Dash into the Crater, Century Magazine,* Sept., 1887, p. 774.

Lee, Guy Carleton: *True Story of the Civil War,* pp. 374–375, Lippincott, Philadelphia, 1903.

Lee, Ronald F.: Letter Re Petersburg Military Park, U. S. Department of the Interior.

McClellan, George B.: *McClellan's Own Story,* Webster, New York, 1887.

McClellan, George B.: *Report on the Organization and Campaigns of the Army of the Potomac,* Sheldon, New York, 1864.

McClure, A. K.: *Abraham Lincoln and Men of War Times,* Times Pub., New York, 1892.

Nolan, J. B., Ed.: *Southeastern Pennsylvania,* Vol. II, pp. 955–1127, Lewis Historical Publishing Company, Inc., Philadelphia and New York, 1943.

Pleasants, Henry, Jr.: *The Tragedy of the Crater,* Christopher, Boston, 1938.

Pleasants, Henry, Jr.: Family Letters, Emma P. Devlin, Brig. Gen. Henry Pleasants, etc.

Powell, William H.: *The Tragedy of the Crater, Century Magazine,* Sept., 1887.

Smith, William Farrar: *Butler's Attack on Drewry's Bluff, Century Magazine,* Sept., 1887, p. 195.

Spalding, W. G.: Address Before Winchester, Mass., Club.

Taylor, Floyd B. (Superintendent, Petersburg National Military Park): Correspondence.

Thomas, Henry Goddard: *The Colored Troops at Petersburg, Century Magazine,* Vol. XXXIV, No. 5, Sept., 1887.

Thompson: *The First Defenders.* (Privately Printed.)
Thompson, Heber S.: *Diary.*
Wood, W. B., and Edmonds, J. S.: *Military History of the Civil War,* Capricorn Books edition, Putnam, New York, 1960.

SPECIAL:

Report of Committee on Conduct of War, 38th Congress, 2nd Session.
Lossing, Benson J.: *The Civil War in America,* Belnap, Hartford, 1866.
Personal Memoirs of P. H. Sheridan, Jenkins and McCowan, New York, 1888.

Index

Marye's Heights, 23
Meade, George Gordon, 32,
    34, 37, 43, 57, 64, 71, 79,
    92, 97, 102, 108, 109,
    112, 122, 131, 133, 134,
    136, 138, 142, 146, 149,
    152, 167
    in investigations, 154, 162,
    163
    letters to Burnside, 79-85
Mifflin, Pennsylvania, 23
Miles, Nelson A., 154
Miner's Journal, The, 16
Mining, in Pottsville, 16, 160
Mississippi, regiments from,
    28
Molly Maguires, The, 15, 166
Monroe, Fortress, 23, 37, 94
Morgan, 24
Morgan's Corner, 151
Morristown, Tennessee, 27
Morton's Battery, 131

Nagle, James, 21
National Battlefield Park, 1
Naveis, Sylvia, 12
Negro division, 90, 91, 102,
    105, 106-108, 110, 112,
    134-137, 142, 145, 163,
    164
New Bern, 21
Newark, 23
Nineteenth Regiment, 106
Ninth Corps, 8, 21, 28, 30, 34,
    35, 37, 38, 39, 43, 78, 91,
    132, 156, 157, 161, 163,
    164
    salient of, 69, 72, 119, 149
Norfolk and Petersburg Rail-
    road, 59

Northern Virginia, Army of,
    140

Ohio, Army of, 23
Ord, Edward O. C., 109, 132,
    137, 155
    in investigation, 162

Pamlico Sound, 21
Pamunkey River, 37
Parks, John G., 54
Pegram, John, 24, 47, 48, 89,
    116, 141
Pemberton, Israel, 12
Peninsular Campaign, 35
Pennsylvania Railroad, 11, 14,
    69
Pennsylvania Regiments:
    27th, 105
    30th, 105
    39th, 105
    43rd, 105
    48th, 1, 8, 18, 30, 33, 104,
    121, 141, 148, 157, 158
Perkins, Joseph G., 106
Perryville, Maryland, 18
Peter's Point, 5
Petersburg, attacks on, 7-8
    founding of, 5
    Park in, 1
Philadelphia, 11, 14, 91, 107,
    150
Philadelphia and Reading Coal
    and Iron Company, 15,
    160, 166
Pittsburgh, 23
Pittsburg & Connellsville Rail-
    road, 11
Plan of assault, 90
Pleasants, Anne (*see* Shaw,
    Anne)

178

Second Brigade, 105, 127, 134
Second Corps, 34, 38, 39, 82, 92, 93, 102, 133, 134, 154
Second Division, 78, 103, 108, 112, 113, 126, 130, 132
Sedgwick, Fort, 157
Seventeenth Regiment, Mississippi, 28
Seventeenth Regiment, South Carolina, 135
Seventh Regiment, Rhode Island, 157
Shaw, Anne, 26, 30, 31, 42, 71, 118, 150, 159, 166
Shaw, Hiram, 25, 30, 159
Sheridan, 92, 93
Sherman, 29
Sigfried, Joshua K., 23, 24, 26, 31, 105, 106, 134, 135, 136
Sixteenth Regiment, Georgia, 28
Sixth Corps, 34, 35, 36, 37, 82
Smith, William Farrar, 7, 34, 37
South Carolina Regiments:
  17th, 135
  18th, 141
  22nd, 141
South Mountain, Battle of, 22
Southwest Grammar School, 13
Spottsylvania, 6, 31, 32
Stanton, Edwin M., 154
Stearns, Ozora P., 105
Stevenson, Thomas G., 112
Stringham, Silas H., 21
Sumter, Fort, 18

Tennessee Regiment, 1st, 24

Tennessee River, 27
Theodolite, use of, 70, 72, 86
Third Division, 103, 108, 112, 113, 127, 128, 130, 131, 143
Thirteenth Regiment, Mississippi, 28
Thirtieth Regiment, Pennsylvania, 105
Thirty-first Regiment, 106
Thirty-ninth Regiment, Pennsylvania, 105
Thomas, Henry Goddard, 106, 134, 135
Toleration Act, 11
Tower Guards, 18
Transportation, through Petersburg, 6
"Traveller," 3, 143
Tunnel, countermining by enemy, 74, 89, 94
  dimensions in, 77, 95
  marl stratum in, 70
  number of men working in, 73, 76
  official attitude toward, 60–62, 66, 85, 121
  removal of dirt from, 60, 73, 87
  time required for, 76
  ventilation problems in, 68–69
  water seepage in, 70, 98, 109
Twenty-eighth Regiment, 106
Twenty-ninth Regiment, 106
Twenty-second Regiment, South Carolina, 141
Twenty-seventh Regiment, Pennsylvania, 105